The Author, A.D. Emery, left secondary school without any academic qualifications. However, whilst playing in a band for some years, he attended evening classes, eventually achieving a BSc in Physics. He started working in engineering, then moved into electromagnetic research, which led him into computer programming. He now lives with his wife, in South Lincolnshire. His children have left home and now live in various parts of the country. Although, the three youngest Grand Children live close, and he enjoys their visits. A passion for writing, despite dyslexia, developed in later years.

To my grandchildren.

A.D. Emery

THE DARSTON REVELATION

AUSTIN MACAULEY PUBLISHERS™

LONDON • CAMBRIDGE • NEW YORK • SHARJAH

A CIP catalogue record for this title is available from the British Library.

ISBN 9781035808755 (Paperback)
ISBN 9781035808762 (ePub e-book)

www.austinmacauley.com

First Published 2024
Austin Macauley Publishers Ltd®
1 Canada Square
Canary Wharf
London
E14 5AA

Ian Rogers Lawrence Bullen for their encouragement for me to keep writing.

This book is for the enjoyment of my grandchildren.

And anyone else who enjoys it.

Chapter 1

Miss Jane Perry was sitting in her front room drinking a cup of tea and looking out of window, having just walked up from the Lower Darston library, where she worked as chief librarian. Her daydreaming was interrupted when a coach full of tourists slowed almost to a standstill, outside the front room window, in order to negotiate the sharp left-hand bend at the bottom of White Swan Hill.

This bend marks the point where the High Street of Lower Darston starts and White Swan Hill ended. Jane watched the coach shunt back and forth, as it struggled around the corner, followed by its subsequent progress down towards The Square.

Another load of Wednesday tourist, she thought to herself. "I wonder why they never come on another day."

The Lane, along which coach had come, was the only direct route to the village of Lower Darston from the Main Road some five miles away. Along its length, the taller trees and bushes growing in its hedges had been sculptured by years of passing traffic, to form a green tunnel just large enough for them to pass through.

In fact, any vehicle larger than a coach would find it virtually impossible to reach Lower Darston, even without the sharp bend at the bottom of White Swan Hill. Larger vehicles had to take the longer route through Upper Darston. White Swan Hill was the name given to the last part of the Lane.

It was not very long, or significantly steep, more of a sudden drop towards the low stone wall opposite. However, this slope combined with the narrowness of both the High Street and White Swan Hill produced a very awkward corner, which proved difficult for all drivers to negotiate, even those with small cars.

Hence, it was not unusual to see part of the stone wall opposite, pushed over, or part of the White Swan pub's boundary wall, which stood on the inside of the corner, badly damaged.

On the outside of the bend stood Jane's house, 'Hill Cottage', which was situated such that if the High Street had continued passed White Swan Hill, it would have gone straight in through the front door.

She had been born in 'Hill Cottage' and lived here all her life. Over the years since her parents had died and left the picturesque thatched cottage to her in their wills, she had endeavoured to maintain it in the pristine condition they had left it, both inside and out. The garden was immaculate, not a weed in sight.

The lawn was trimmed to just the right length and the front hedge always looked as if it had just been cut, which in itself was a direct result of the tourist trade.

Her mind drifted back over the years, several years ago, when she had decided to replace the original wooden paling fence, which bordered along White Swan Hill, with a hedge, after one of the coaches had demolished the fence whilst trying to negotiate the bend, having decided that a hedge would survive encounters with motor vehicles much better than the original fence. Fortunately, her judgement had been proved correct on many occasions since.

Dragging her mind back to the present day, she continued watching, as the latest arrival progressed down the High Street and imagined the tour-guide standing up after they had rounded the White Swan Hill bend, and giving-out gems of information to her captive audience, who were usually Americans.

The tour-guide's script went something like, "As we come into the village of Lower Darston, you can see over there on the right, beyond the fields, the fifteenth century church of St John the Baptist. You will be able to see it better on our guided tour tomorrow morning. We are currently in the High Street, which continues down to the Square, where the library is located, it's that imposing building directly in front of us."

The guide turned and pointed through the windscreen. In unison, all the passenger's heads craned to see out the front of the coach.

"When we get to the library, the road turns sharp right and becomes the Lower High Street, which then continues down to the bridge over the River Darant. Can you see where the two High Streets meet in front of the library?"

Again, heads stretched to see.

"They also form two sides of what is now called the Square. Sometime in the past, it was the village's market square, but unfortunately, the market itself has been transferred to the larger village of Upper Darston. As you will see in a moment, in the centre of the Square is a grand Victorian Market Clock, which is all that remains of the once flourishing market."

Having got into the spirit the thing, the guide continued, "You will notice the library is built at such an angle that it not only faces into the Square, but you can also see up the High Street and at the same time down Lower High Street. Apparently, so the story goes, a rich gentleman who wanted to settle in the village built it, which was during the time George III was on the throne."

"Unfortunately, he had a very nosy wife and it was at her insistence that the house was built at that strange angle, in order for her to be able to see everything that was going on, in all three directions at the same time. The rumour has it that she could perform her information gathering from every room at the front of the house."

"After the couple died, the house was sold and eventually, after changing hands many times, was taken over by the County Council, who turned it into the local library and museum. You will be able to see more of it on our tour tomorrow."

By now, the coach had pulled over to the west side of the Square, coming to a halt in front of the entrance of 'The Crown Hotel'. Thus bringing the tour-guide's monologue to a close.

This was the third hotel on their tour, which meant all the passengers knew what the procedure would be. At the instant, the coach stopped, everyone grabbed their hand luggage and disgorged themselves out from the coach, following the guide through the hotel entrance into the vestibule. Just like a group of school children scrambling to follow their teacher.

There had always been an inn or hotel of some description on this site in Lower Darston, from as far back as local records went. The present building, on this site, dated from around the eighteen century, with many additions having been appended to it over the years, although, some of the modifications had done little to improve its appearance or functionality.

Stepping through the front door of the hotel, was like entering the film set of some historic gothic epic, with its dark oak panelling and massive beams across the ceiling. The large staircase at the far end of the vestibule had carved Heraldic Beasts, holding shields and guarding the end of each banister, whilst, numerus shields sporting Coats-of-Arms, were hanging around the walls.

John Jones, the village knew him as 'JJ', and his wife, Evelyn, who were the current proprietors of 'The Crown Hotel', methodically registered and dispatched their new visitors off in the appropriate direction towards whatever room they had been allocated. 'JJ' and Evelyn smiled benignly as the passengers, who were enthralled by the gothic splendour before them, exclaiming in heavy American accents, about the wonders of old historic buildings.

Various groups formed and discussed the merits of this hotel, compared with the others they had stayed at, on the tour so far. The main thrust of the conversations concentrated on evaluating the quantity and size of the beams, oak panelling and similar items.

Three quarters of an hour later, relative calm had returned to the reception area.

"You know, that's unusual," murmured John thoughtfully, as he looked at the register, whilst tidying the reception desk.

"What's that?" Evelyn replied.

"During all the years we have been having these weekly coaches, I don't think we have ever had any English people on them before. This time we've got two."

"Are they together?"

"Well, they're booked into separate single rooms."

"Let me see the register—Ms Caroline Dobbs and Mr Julian Drake—well at least it's not Mr and Mrs Smith!"

"I know, they're secret lovers and their parents have forbidden them to see each other, so they have come on this tour together," Evelyn chuckled.

"Don't be silly!" Her husband admonished. "You've been reading too many books. Anyway, you wouldn't get much time alone on these tours."

Chapter 2

The Market Clock struck four o'clock.

By this time, most of the visitors had decided to walk to one or more of the various points of interest scattered around Lower Darston. However, because it was Wednesday afternoon, early closing day, it would be inevitable that the majority would end up at Anne's tea room, which stood next to the hotel, simply because of one simple reason; it was the only place in the village that was open on a Wednesday afternoon.

Lower Darston kept its early closing Wednesday as if it were a religious festival.

Caroline stood waiting at the bottom of the hotel staircase. After a few moments, Julian joined her.

"It's dead in here," he whispered, looking round the bar and reception area. "Where would you like to go? Although I'm not sure what's open. This place seems to be shut up like a clam."

"Ye Olde Worlde tea room next door is open. I noticed it when I looked out of my bedroom window whilst I was unpacking."

"Ok, let's go there then. We may even get a cup of coffee, if we sit quietly and don't upset any of the old biddies. I expect it'll be full of them, that sort of place always is."

"First one there chooses the table," Caroline called over her shoulder, as she bounced out through the open front door into the Square.

Julian followed at a more leisurely pace and by the time he had reached the door of Anne's, Caroline was already sitting at a table next to the window, overlooking the Square. As he strolled over to the table, he whispered in Caroline's ear, "I told you it would be full of old biddies, look they are all watching us. It makes me feel as if we're intruding into their private personal world."

"Shush, be quiet and don't be so silly. Anyway, if you look, they are all from the coach. I expect all the locals are at home, its Wednesday, remember. Look here comes the waitress, what would you like to drink?"

"Just a coffee."

"I'm having a scone as well. Do you want one?"

"Ok"

"Can I help you?" The waitress asked, as she reached their table.

"Yes. Can we have two coffees, with milk instead of cream, and two scones with jam and butter, please?"

"Anything else?"

"No, thank you."

The waitress moved off towards another table, which had just filled up with some other passengers from the coach.

Caroline and Julian sat looking out of the window.

After a few moments silence, Caroline commented, "It looks different to how I remember it, it seems smaller somehow. I mean, I don't even remember this place."

"Yes, I know what you are getting at, but we were only six and seven years old at the time, and when you're small everything seems bigger than it really is. And that, may I remind you, was twenty years ago, which is an awfully long time."

"Hmm, I suppose you're right," murmured Caroline, still looking out of the window. "Look there! The cake shop next to the library, I remember that."

"Yes, so do I," agreed Julian, after he had taken in the detail of the window's outlook, for the first time. "If I remember correctly, we used to get an iced-bun each, after having been to the library with Nan on pension day. It's strange how it seems such a long time ago in one way, all vague and misty. Yet when some of it comes back, the rest seems to click into place as if it happened yesterday."

At that point, the waitress brought their coffee and scones over to them.

"Have you seen anyone you recognise yet?" Julian asked, after the waitress had left. He watched as Caroline's eyes scanned round the room.

"Not yet. Although, I don't think we will today, it's Wednesday."

"I'm not sure we would anyway, every one we knew or who knew us must be ancient by now. That's if they are not dead."

Julian's thoughts drifted back over the years.

"I know!" Caroline interjected suddenly, returning Julian back to the present with a jolt. "Let's go and see if we can find

Nan's old house? It can't be far from here, because, as I remember it, we used to walk everywhere then."

"Ok. If you think you can remember where it is, and how to get there," replied Julian.

Having finished their coffee and scones, Julian went over to the till and paid the bill, whilst Caroline went outside to wait for him.

"Where shall we start?" Caroline mooted, after Julian had joined her outside.

"Cross over to the library," replied Julian, "and let's try and get things into perspective first. Seeing things from the right angle may help to trigger our memories a bit more."

They walked across the Square and stood in front of the library, surveying the area where they had just been standing.

"The colours on the Market Clock look brighter than I remember them," remarked Caroline.

"They always paint that sort of thing in bright colours, it's to keep the tourists happy," condescended Julian.

"But we are tourists," smirked Caroline.

"Ok! Ok!" He smiled. "I'd forgotten," and gave her a friendly shove. "Anyway, I think Anne's tea room must be new, well at least less than twenty years old. But I can't remember what was there before. What about you?"

"No, I can only recall the hotel being on that side of the Square. Just a building with that large Crown over the door, as it is now. Maybe Anne's was part of the hotel back then— I don't know."

"The old post office is still there. I wonder if—O' what was her name—is still running it. You know, the short round dumpy woman. She and Nan used to jabber on for ages about this, that and the other."

"I know who you mean, she would give us sweets and let us read the comics on the paper counter, to keep us happy whilst Nan and her gossiped. We must go in there tomorrow, when it's open, to see if she's still there. You never know, she may even recognise us."

"Isn't it frustrating when you cannot remember things. Now what was her name? It just won't come."

"If I remember correctly," said Caroline, pointing down the Lower High Street, "we used to come up from somewhere down there. Past the Ironmongers over there, it always had a load of bright new dustbins outside. Then past the antique shop, that's been smartened up a bit, from the old junk shop it was."

"Then we would go into the post office and after coming out of there, we would cross over and turn into the Square and into the library."

"For yet another good gossip with the library lady," interrupted Julian. "I remember her name—Miss Parker; no, Penny, Perry—that was it Miss Perry. She's probably still there, I always felt she owned the library, the way she used to fuss over the books and make us keep quiet."

"Have you finished?"

"Sorry."

"Then as you said earlier, we went into the cake shop next door and had a bun each. Then…"

"Well?"

"You interrupting me, it's made me forget. My mind has gone completely blank," said Caroline with frustration.

"Never mind," consoled Julian. "As far as I can remember, Nan just did her ordinary shopping after that. You know butchers, grocers, greengrocers and the like. Working her way back down Lower High Street."

The pair of them sat on the low stonewall in front of the library, half thinking and half dreaming, in the warm afternoon sun.

After ten minutes or so, Julian suddenly stood up. "Come on! If you can remember coming up Lower High Street with Nan, then Nan's old house must be down there somewhere."

Caroline got up and they both dawdled their way down the left-hand side of Lower High Street, looking in the various shop windows, trying to recall how their contents and displays had looked when they last saw them. Eventually, they arrived at the corner of Love Lane. Opposite Love Lane, on the other side of Lower High Street, was Church Lane.

After a pause, Caroline said, "I'm sure Nan's house is along there," and pointed to Church Lane.

They crossed over Lower High Street and started walking along the right-hand side of Church Lane. This side of the lane consisted of a grassy verge, with a shallow ditch situated about two feet from the edge of the road. Beyond the ditch, was a small bank, on the top of which where the remnants of a Hawthorn hedge.

On the opposite side of the lane, stood a row of terraced houses, numbering one to six. Number one was at the corner of Lower High Street and Church Lane with the rest numbered sequentially along Church Lane. According to the ornately carved stone plaque on the wall between numbers three and four, the houses apparently dated from 1853.

They were long low double fronted cottage style houses, with the windows of their upper rooms peering out from just below the overhanging roof. At the start of their lives, they were probably thatched, but now had grey Welsh Slates on their roofs.

Church Lane had a gentle left-hand curve to it, which lasted the length of the terrace, before continuing up towards the Church, about mile further on. Because of the curve in the lane, you couldn't see the front of number six until you had passed number three.

Caroline stopped opposite where numbers five and six joined each other.

"I think it was number five."

"Go on a bit further," urged Julian.

They had walked about fifty yards beyond the end of the terrace, before Julian stopped and looked back at the end gable of number six.

"Yes, I think you're right," he said. "There's the alley-way, which runs along the back of the houses. When we came to Nan's, we always went in the second door along the alley."

They sat on top of the bank, in a gap between the depleted Hawthorn bushes. By now, the Sun had lost some of its heat and the day had turned into a very pleasant summer's evening. Birds had started to sing their evensong, in the trees lining the bank of the river Darant.

The back gardens, of the terraced houses, extended a hundred yards or so, down a gentle slope almost to the bank of the river.

"There the old school." Julian pointed across the river towards where they could see the Lower High Street continuing beyond the bridge over the river.

Then he added in philosophical voice, "You know, it's a shame that only people who have high incomes or have lived here for ages, can afford to live in villages like this."

After a few more moments of silence, Julian glanced down at his watch. "Come on. We had better be getting back. It's ten to eight and dinner started at seven thirty, which means we won't get any if we're not back before nine."

Hurriedly, they started to retrace their steps. As they reached the corner of Lower High Street, Julian voiced his thoughts.

"I'm sure someone was watching us from number three."

"I noticed the curtains moving," replied Caroline, "but I thought it was a draft or the wind. I wonder who could be interested in us."

"Probably just some old biddy wanting to know who had the audacity to trespass in her lane," retorted Julian.

They briskly walked back to the hotel.

Dinner for the coach party, was from the fixed price menu. On Wednesdays, this consisted of: roast lamb, with roasted potatoes and mint sauce, mashed potatoes, cabbage and peas. Followed by ice cream or gateau, and finally coffee.

After taking their place at the dining table, dinner duly arrived and the various courses followed in quick succession. Thanks to the experience of the waitresses who had been trained to deal with large numbers, in a short space of time.

Julian and Caroline sat drinking their coffee.

"What do you think of the old village so far?" Julian asked.

"It was all right, until we went and found Nan's old house, since then I've had a funny feeling of foreboding. It's probably an attack of nostalgia. I can't help wondering who's living in her house now."

"We could find out tomorrow at the library if you want to, from the electoral lists," replied Julian. "Anyway, I have just remembered who used to live next door to Nan, at number six, it was the old Verger." And then added thoughtfully, "I wonder if he is still alive?"

After draining the coffee from his cup, Julian stood up and as if dismissing the events of the day, said, "I'm going to watch tele' before going to bed. Coming?"

"No," replied Caroline. "My mind's going round and round. I think I'll just go straight to bed."

Chapter 3

Clear early morning Sun streamed through the trees surrounding the back garden of 'Hill Cottage', producing a dappled mosaic of light and dark on the back lawn. The period between May and September was the only time in the year when the warming rays of the Sun could reach round and shine on the back of the cottage, and that only occurred in the early morning or late evening.

Today, the sunrise had been almost due northeast, and having climbed above the trees, its light now shone obliquely through the leaded glass of the back bedroom windows. Projecting an illuminated area of brilliant diamond shaped patches onto the bedroom wall.

Jane usually slept with the windows open during the summer months, and last night had been no exception. This allowed the pleasant sound of the early morning birds, as they welcomed the new day, to drift into the bedroom.

After returning from the bathroom, Jane put on a dark skirt, white blouse, which tied at the neck with large floppy bow, and a jacket to match the skirt. This outfit she considered her working uniform and had always worn this style for work. It somehow seemed to be in harmony with the atmosphere of the library, where she worked.

Anyway, she could not see the point of changing after all these years, although, as had been pointed out to her on one particular occasion, in some circles it would be considered old fashioned. However, the look Jane had given the person making the comment, had ensured there would certainly not be any more comments of that nature in the future.

She possessed her working uniform in several different colours; dark blue, black and dark grey. Today, it was the turn of the dark grey ensemble.

Standing in front of the long dressing mirror on the wall, she adjusted her bow and combed her iron-grey hair into its normal style. At one time, she had hoped her hair would go completely white, but as the quantity of white hair increased, it never went beyond the stage where it gave an overall iron-grey colour.

However, with the passage of time, she had come to terms with the stern countenance that hair colouring gave her. The thought of using a bottle to change the colouring of her hair to a shade she felt would be more in keeping with her temperament, did not appeal to her one bit.

Having finished dressing, Jane went down stairs into the living room and drew back the curtains. Then passed through into the kitchen, which was at the back of the cottage, to prepare her breakfast.

Whilst waiting for the toast to brown and the kettle to boil, she switched on the radio to listen to the seven o'clock news. The reported happenings were probably very important and interesting to the nation as a whole, but the majority of the items usually failed to arouse any significant interest in Jane.

On the other hand, she did feel it was part of her job, as a librarian, to be aware of the general outline of what had been deemed news worthy that day; because, she felt she should be in a position to provide superficial, although noncommittal, answers to the questions her clientele at the library may ask, concerning whatever item of the day's news had caught their interest. Most outsiders would call it gossip.

After pouring the boiling water into the teapot, she placed it (covered with its woolly tea cosy) onto a tray, with a cup and saucer (bone china with small pale blue roses round the outside), the milk jug (semi-skimmed), several slices of toast (whole meal), some butter (soft spread margarine), and finally a pot of marmalade (home-made from the church bazaar).

Once the preparations were completed, Jane took the tray out onto the patio and settled herself down at the square wooden table, which was positioned so she could look out over the back lawn. During the short summer period, when the sun's rays could reach this part of the garden, she liked to eat her breakfast on the patio as many time as the weather would permit her.

'Hill cottage' had been Jane's birthplace and had enjoyed a happy, carefree childhood. Although, her parents had not been poor, Jane could remember being aware of occasions when it had been difficult for them to make ends meet.

Her father had been senior librarian at the library, here in Lower Darston, back in the days when it had a staff of six. After Jane left school, she managed to secure a junior position at the same library. Slowly working herself up the promotion ladder until, after her father's death, she was promoted to senior librarian.

Each step on the ladder had been won by hard work and merit alone, her father made certain she didn't attain it by being the boss's daughter. Unfortunately, numerous economy drives and cut-backs over the years, had eventually reduced the staff of six down to its present level of one librarian, Jane, and a part-time helper.

Mr Perry, Jane's father, had died when Jane was twenty-eight years old and shortly after his death, Mrs Perry became terminally ill. Jane nursed her mother for three years, caring for her needs single handed, until she died. Being an only child, all her parents' possessions, including 'Hill Cottage' and gardens, became hers.

In addition, and to her pleasant surprise, over the years her parents had managed to accumulate a significant amount of savings. This legacy proved large enough to provide her with financial security. As a result, she was no longer dependent on her meagre salary from the library.

This enabled her to live comfortably, with the eager consent of the local authority, because it meant they could get away with paying her a smaller salary than they would have had to pay otherwise. Anyway, it provided Jane with a way of life she found very satisfying.

Over the years, many suitors had beaten a path to Jane's front door, but none had proved to be Mr Right, in Jane's eyes anyway. Some of the men thought they were God's gift to women and were extremely disappointed when Jane failed to prostrate herself at their feet. Others thought that by taking her to a pub on a Saturday night and then spending the whole evening drinking, was showing a girl a good time.

Although, that was an improvement on the men who thought, she should be taking them out for a meal; once one took her out to a restaurant and ordered two beers to go with the meal instead of a bottle of wine (Jane liked a bit of sophistication when she is taken out).

However, there was one gentleman who lasted a whole five dates, and Jane had started to consider him as a possibility, but then half way through the main course, whilst they were having a meal in a restaurant, he suddenly said, "I think it's time that you paid for this meal."

Jane didn't bat an eye lid, she continued eating her meal in silence, once she had finished eating her main course, she stood up, collected her coat, and walked out of the restaurant and flagged down a taxi to take her home. Jane never saw the man again.

As Jane got older, there was the occasional man who thought that at her age, she would be desperate for any man, but they were wrong, and they didn't even get a date.

Consequently, she had remained single. Finding, as the years passed, she enjoyed her maiden-hood and the solitude it afforded her when she was at home, plus the freedom to socialise with or visit who ever she pleased in the wide circle of friends she had built up over the years.

Chapter 4

Caroline had been given a bedroom situated in the front left-hand corner of the Hotel, on the first floor. One of her bedroom windows had been built into the end wall of the building, in addition to the one facing the front.

Consequently, one window faced south, overlooking the Square, and the other which faced east, overlooked the entrance to Anne's tea room, because it lay further back from the Square than the front of the Hotel.

After making herself a cup of coffee, with the hot drink facilities in her room, Caroline climbed back into bed and sipping her drink and enjoyed the morning sunshine streaming through the windows.

Breakfast, for their coach party, would not start being served until eight thirty, which gave her about an hour to pamper herself and get dressed at an unaccustomed leisurely pace. It also gave her time to meditate on the happenings of yesterday.

Had she and Julian been right in coming back to the village? When they planned the visit, which was about six months ago, only the happy times had been remembered. The thought of seeing places where they had had once played as children, had been fired by the nostalgic memories of happiness.

But, for an instant, all Caroline could remember was the sadness and trauma associated with their original leaving. Although, it was twenty years ago, she still felt tears welling up in her eyes at the thought of Nan dying, the finality of the funeral and her and Julian being separated and taken away from the village to live with different uncles in the south of England.

Amidst all the sudden emotional turmoil inside her mind, she could again hear the supposed words of comfort echoing around inside her head.

"Don't cry, love, it's all for the best."

"You'll soon forget all this upset."

"It's best you go away from here."

"Julian will only be just down the road; you will be able to see him whenever you want."

It turned out that Julian was twenty miles 'just down the road' and the promised frequent visits very soon became less and less. Fortunately, both uncles had encouraged them to write to each other. Consequently, as the frequency of their visits became less, the more they communicated their thoughts and dreams to each other through letters.

This continued until both of them had left their respective foster homes and setup their own flats. The enforced estrangement during their childhood had resulted in Julian and her becoming very close and protective towards one another.

Caroline smiled to herself as she thought of protecting Julian, suddenly the reciprocal thought of Julian protecting her, felt very reassuring.

"Are you awake in there?" Julian's voice suddenly intruded into Caroline's thoughts, as he banged on her door of her room.

"Yes…err yes, I'm about to get dressed," she stammered back at him.

"Don't be too long about it, or you will miss breakfast. I'll see you down stairs."

In the tour brochure, the itinerary for Lower Darston went as follows:

- Two nights stop at 'The Crown Hotel', which is a seventeenth century coaching inn, situated in the charming village of Lower Darston. All rooms have private facilities and a kettle for making tea and coffee drinks.

- We arrive Wednesday afternoon—this is free for you to explore the village (please note this is also early closing day for the village). Dinner starts being served at eight o'clock.

- Thursday morning is for you to obtain any shopping or souvenirs of your visit. The afternoon tour will take you round the fifteenth century church and then the local library and museum. Again, dinner starts at eight o'clock.

- On Friday morning, after a leisurely breakfast, we leave for our next stop (A full English breakfast is available on both mornings, at no extra cost).

Breakfast was being served in the oak panelled dining room. Each of the hotel rooms had been allocated a separate table. However, the guests in the single rooms, as there was only six of them, had been grouped together on one large table.

Julian dexterously rearranged the room numbers on the table, so he and Caroline were sitting together at one end of it.

Julian had just started his cornflakes, when Caroline joined him at the table.

"Help yourself to orange-juice, cornflakes, or whatever you fancy, from that table over there. They will then come and take the rest of your order," Julian told her.

The cooked part of their breakfast duly arrived. Both of them ate in silence, watching the various comings and goings of the staff and guests in the dining room.

"What would you like to do this morning?" Julian asked, as he started his toast. "We can leave going to the library until this afternoon, as we are going there on the guided tour. The tour leaves here at twelve thirty and it's about quarter past nine now, so that gives us about three hours to explore the village."

"I would like to go to the post office; just to see if that little rotund woman who used to run it is still there," replied Caroline.

"Sounds ok to me."

"O' and please let's go and get some iced buns from the cake shop, the one next to the library, where we used to get them when we were little. Just to see if they still taste as good as I remember."

Julian smiled at her, like an indulgent uncle giving way to some outrageous request. Eventually, they finished drinking their tea, and strolled outside into the Square.

"Post office first, I think, it's too close to breakfast for iced buns," Julian said with a grin, and turned towards the post office.

"It's rather crowded in here," remarked Caroline, on reaching the post office door.

"I expect it's full of all those old biddies, we were sure would have been in Anne's, yesterday afternoon," retorted Julian. "I know why! It's Thursday, everyone must be getting their pension."

Darston post office was a long narrow shop. The counter, which had been partition off at one end for use as the post office, was situated at the opposite end of the shop, to the entrance through which they had just come.

Along both sides and down the centre were racks and shelves crammed full of magazines, comics, post-cards, newspapers, packets of biscuits, tins of this and that; in fact, everything you would normally expect to find in a corner shop, plus a lot more.

"It doesn't look any different to how I remember it," whispered Caroline.

"I think most of this stuff has been here for all the years we've been away," replied Julian.

"Excuse me!" a rotund old age pensioner asked, as she squeezed past them and went down the gap between the racks, followed by a large shopping trolley on wheels and a scrawny man, who was obviously her husband; and joined the queue of other pensioners waiting to be served at the post-office end of the shop.

Julian started to look through the post-cards, while Caroline went over to the comics and started to browse through them.

"If you want to read them, why don't buy them? I think a quarter of an hour is long enough to choose, don't you?" The woman serving behind the post office counter shouted across to Caroline.

Caroline, who had become so engrossed in the comics, that she hadn't noticed the passage of time, spun round and stared at the woman glaring at her from behind the portioning.

"You tourists are all the same," continued the woman. "Spend hours looking but don't buy anything, just getting in the way of regular customers who live in the village."

By now, everyone in the shop was looking at Caroline, as a result she went scarlet, opened her mouth to reply but for some reason, she didn't know what, decided against it and strode outside.

A few moments later, Julian joined her clutching a post-card.

"I had to buy something after that outburst, didn't I?" He said grinning at her. "Anyway, that wasn't like you to be lost for words, in that sort of confrontation."

"Cantankerous old so and so!" Caroline snapped indignantly. "That wasn't the woman who used to gossip with Nan, she wouldn't have minded how long we spent looking at the comics."

"Come on, I'll buy you that iced bun you wanted, perhaps it'll calm you down and cheer you up."

They crossed over the Square and stood outside the cake shop next to the library.

"I'll wait here," Caroline said, looking through the shop window. "I don't want to be shouted at again."

"Ok."

Caroline watched Julian through the shop window as he joined the queue and eventually purchased the iced buns.

"Shall we sit over there and, eat them, on those seats round the base of the clock tower," suggested Julian, after he came out.

They crossed over to the small island in the centre of the Square on which the clock tower stood. Two old age pensioners were seated on the west side that faced the post office, deep in conversation. Consequently, they selected the south bench which faced the library.

The sun beat down on them as they as they devoured their buns, even though the sky was a pleasant summer blue, it wasn't clear and had several white fluffy clouds, slowly drifting across it.

"Do they meet with your approval?" Julian asked, after they had finished eating them.

"Yes. I feel much better. Come on, I'll buy you a drink in Anne's while we wait for the coach."

Having ordered their coffee, they sat staring out the window.

After several minutes, Caroline said in a faraway voice, "Julian, do you think we have done the right thing coming to the village? On a day like this, I find it difficult to imagine how anything unpleasant could have ever happened here."

"Yes, I think we have done the right thing, because if we hadn't come, we would have always been wondering what had really happened in the past. I'm expecting there may be somethings that we both will find unpleased."

"Our memories are distorted, due to the fact that we were so young at the time; and inevitably, many of the people involved would have not revealed the truth to us at that time, on the misconception that they were being kind, and in some cases, no doubt quench the nagging guilt that was building up inside their brains."

"I'm sure you are right, but I do hope that what we eventually discover will quell the anxiety and sadness I feel from time to time when memories of the events flood their way through my mind."

"Remember, most of the people involved at that time are probably dead. Also we are not using our original name and the way we look will have changed over the twenty or so years since we were last here. Consequently, I feel sure that no one will recognise us. At worst, if someone does recognise us they will not know why we are familiar to them."

"I'm sure you are right, but I still worry about those doubts that flood across my mind when my mind recalls the past. I just don't want the sadness that comes with the memories, to keep returning."

"Over time, they will slowly fade and eventually stop."

Chapter 5

The tour bus arrived outside the hotel at twelve fifteen and the majority of visitors, including Julian and Caroline, boarded it for the afternoon tour.

"Thank you all for joining our conducted tour this afternoon," said the tour-guide, as the coach moved off. "I'm sure you will find it an interesting experience. Our first stop is the fifteenth century church, St John the Baptist. It should only take us five to ten minutes to get there."

The coach approached the church along Church Lane. Julian and Caroline watched as they passed the six terraced houses, where their Nan had once lived. Further up, they passed a large building on the left called 'Bank House' and on the right hand side of the lane, next to the church, stood the Vicarage.

Opposite the church, the local council had provided a gravelled area for cars and coaches to park, which the coach pulled onto.

"In about fifteen minutes, at one o'clock, the Reverend Paul Jones will be giving a short talk about the history of the church and some of the people who have been associated with it in the past. I'm sure you will find it very interesting. Please will you all be back on the coach by one forty-five, ready to leave for our next stop," announced the guide. "Enjoy your visit."

All the passengers disembarked from the coach and wandered towards the church. Julian and Caroline paused in the porch, where a notice informed them the talk would be held in the Vestry.

A small exhibition of artefacts associated with the church and village was on display in the Bell Ringing Chamber situated at the base of the tower. The six bell ropes, which would normally have been hanging down in the centre of the room, forming a circle, were hooked onto a round wooden disc, which was about four feet in diameter.

This had been hosted up to the ceiling, with the aid of a rope that was attached to the disc's centre and passed over a series of pulleys and secured on a cleat screwed to the white washed wall. The way in which the red, white and green Sallies looped down, made the whole thing looked like a giant spider waiting to drop from the ceiling.

Various display cabinets had been arranged against three of the walls, with several peal boards and a row of coat hooks confined to the fourth. The centre of the room had been kept clear, so that the bell ringers could perform without getting tangled up with the display items.

The majority of the exhibits consisted of old documents and manuscripts written by various notorieties from the village and surrounding area, usually bequeathing sums of money or property to the church.

After working their way round the displays, Julian and Caroline made their way down the aisle towards the Vestry door, which was located in the north wall, just in front of the alter rail.

Inside the Vestry, six rows of chairs were set out, facing a projection screen. A slide projector had been mounted on a shelf attached to the wall above the door they had just come through. Standing next to the projection screen, stood a man, who was about six-foot-tall, well built, but not fat, with a full head of white hair.

Caroline noted his eyebrows looked black in contrast to brightness of his Crowning Glory and concluded he once had very dark, if not black hair.

"From his 'Dog Collar', I would say he is the Vicar," whispered Caroline, as she and Julian sat in the third row from the front.

"I hope this talk doesn't sound too much like a Sunday sermon," whispered Julian in reply.

Over the next few minutes, several of the other visitors filed in and took their seats.

"It's one o'clock, so I think we will make a start," said the Reverend Paul Jones. His voice was full and mellow, with a slight hint of some indistinguishable accent. Certainly not the sort of voice you would expect from a country Vicar.

"This church, Saint John the Baptist, was founded in fourteen eighty-seven, by a small group of local monks. The original building is the section in which the side-altar is now located. It's on the south side of the church, running from about level with the main altar, back to the wall of the entrance porch."

"You will notice the roof beams are much lower than those on the north side. When it was originally built, experts estimate it was probably big enough for a congregation about twenty parishioners. This first slide shows an artist impression of how it may have looked."

The Reverend Jones pressed the remote control, and the first slide flashed onto the screen.

The audience listened with apparent interest as the talk progressed. Firstly, the history of the building itself was out lined. Then came the various royal patrons, who had been associated with the church.

Next, the names of the deceased persons who had, at one time or another, held positions of influence in the village and had given money or property to the church, in order to appease their conscience (most of the names mentioned, Julien and Caroline recognised from the documents on display in the exhibition). Finally, the Reverend Jones mentioned some of the mysteries associated with the church.

"The most recent unsolved mystery is that of 'The Hanging Banker'."

"About twenty-four or even twenty-five years ago, the local banker was found, so the rumour goes, hanging from one of the bell ropes. You may have noticed the ropes hanging up in the Bell Ringing Chamber; it's the room in which our small exhibition is set out at the moment, that's where he was found."

"Unfortunately, the police could not establish if it was an accident, suicide or murder. There weren't any clues or evidence, to indicate one way or another. Unfortunately, his wife also died suddenly, about six months later. I expect we shall never know what really happened."

"And that, Ladies and Gentlemen, brings me to the end of my talk. Thank you for listening. If you have enjoyed the talk, and would like to show your appreciation, please make a donation to the church restoration fund. You will find a contribution box next to the entrance on the way out."

"I knew he would want money for something," muttered Julian, as they left the Vestry and walked up the ails towards the door leading to the outside.

"I think he put a lot of work into preparing that talk," conceded Caroline. "I enjoyed it, so I'm going to put some money in the box."

"Ok, that's up to you. Though that mystery of 'The Swinging Banker' seems familiar, for some reason."

By now, they had emerged from the porch, into the grave yard. Caroline sat down on a large tabular tombstone and surveyed the outside of the church.

"That account is really getting to me," Julian said, half to himself and half to Caroline.

"Why is that?" She replied.

"I don't know why! If I did, it wouldn't be getting at me, would it?" He snapped back.

"We better get back on the coach, most of the others are back already," said Caroline, after a few moments silence.

After the last of the passengers had re-joined the coach. The guide announced, "Our next stop is the library and local museum. As this is located opposite the hotel where we are staying, the coach will park outside the hotel, and we will walk across to the library."

Eventually, the coach arrived back outside the Crown hotel. After disembarking, the passengers crossed the Square and followed the tour guide into the library. Most of the ground floor was taken up by the lending library, which was reached by passing through a glass door located on the left, as you came in through the main front door.

Directly opposite the entrance stood what was once the main staircase of the original house, though now it bore many scars because of being used, or rather misused, by the general public. Although, the striking grandeur it originally had when it was constructed could still be appreciated. On the right, standing in the doorway of the library's administration offices, stood Jane Perry.

As the passengers started filling the hallway, Jane moved across to the stairs and stood several steps up from the bottom, so she could see over the heads of the group.

"Welcome to Lower Darston's Library and Local Museum. My name is Jane Perry and I'm the chief librarian here," Jane announced, after the last of the passengers had squeezed in.

"As you can see," she continued, "the main lending library occupies most of the ground floor. The first floor is partly taken up by the reference library and partly by the museum, which also occupies the whole of the second floor. Would you please follow me?"

Jane started to ascend the stairs and the group followed.

Pausing at the top of the stairs, she continued, "We were very fortunate when the council took over this house, which I hasten to add was long before my time, because during the conversion, they decided to keep the original rooms as they were, and also kept the structural changes to a minimum."

"Although the décor is not what it was, as you wander round the museum, you find the atmosphere of the original house can still be felt."

By now, Jane followed by our tour guide and the passengers had entered what was the upper drawing room.

"Ladies and Gentlemen, I'm going to give you a short resume of the history attached to the house, then an outline of some of the interesting artefacts contained in the museum itself, after which, you can browse round at your leisure."

Jane regurgitated the standard spiel reserved for the Wednesday tourists. It was the same speech she had given to hundreds of previous groups, who had visited the museum before.

"She's as commanding as ever; look, everyone is hanging on her every word," whispered Julien, who had recovered from his earlier grumpiness.

"I'm sure she hasn't change one bit," Caroline whispered in reply.

After ten minutes or so, the speech came to an end and the group started to disperse into the various rooms and galleries.

Having meandered through several rooms of displays, Julian and Caroline found themselves looking at a wall covered in pictures. In the centre of the wall were two, larger than life, full length pictures of a man and woman. These, so the caption stated, were the original owners of the house.

On each side of these central pair, were other portraits interspersed with landscapes of views around the village. One in particular drew Julian's attention.

"Caroline, isn't that the big house we passed in the coach on the way to the church earlier?"

Caroline examined the watercolour. "The notice underneath describes it as a view of Bank-House, painted by an unknown artist in about 1930."

"Do you recognise it?" A voice interrupted.

They both spun round to find Jane Perry standing behind them. "You are Julian and Caroline, aren't you?" She asked.

"Yes, I'm Julian Drake and this is Caroline Dobbs. Why?"

"Why should we remember the house in this painting?" Caroline asked, frowning. "Surely, it's only familiar because we passed it on the way to the church a few hours ago?"

Before Jane could answer their question, two other members of the tourist group wandered in to the room and also started to look at the paintings.

"Look, the library closes in about half an hour at five, and I have several things I must do before then." Jane said, looking at her watch. "Continue your look round the museum until just before five, then come downstairs and wait for me in the entrance. I think there are several things you should know, and it will be easier to tell you without the threat of possible interruption."

Chapter 6

It was about five minutes before five o'clock, when Julian and Caroline made their way back towards the entrance of the library. Most of the coach party had already left, and the remaining stragglers were making their way back to the Hotel opposite. Jane eventually appeared, ushering the last of the public out from the lending library section and, after they had passed into the Square, she closed the front door.

"Would you please check the rest of the building is empty, you can then go home. I'm not going yet, so I'll lock up when I have finished," Jane called to the other librarian, who was working in the lending section. Then, turning to Julian and Caroline, added, "Would you like to come through to my office?"

They followed Jane through the doorway marked 'Private', where they had seen her standing on their arrival. This lead into a room with its walls painted in a very pale yellow, which was obviously used as a general office for the library staff. In the centre of the room were two desks, placed facing each other.

On the desks and the floor next to them, stood numerous piles of books with various labels and slips of paper sticking out from among their pages. Also, a considerable number of wallet folders were stacked along where the two desks abutted each other.

Attached to the wall opposite where they were standing was a shelf, which ran the whole length of the room and supported a multitude of box-files, ring-binders and yet more books. A second door in the left hand wall, carried the legend 'Chief Librarian'. Jane opened it, and bid them enter.

This inner office appeared to be about the same size as the outer office, but where the outer office gave an air of chaos, here was neatness and order. It was occupied by a single desk, slightly larger than the two in the outer office, with an executive type swivel chair behind it; three four-draw filling cabinets, two padded upright chairs and a bookcase containing about thirty or so books, plus a low table.

"Please sit down," said Jane, indicating the two upright chairs. She closed the door, and went round to sit behind her desk.

"Why should we know about that house?" Immediately clamoured Julian and Caroline in unison.

"Why are you interested in us after all this time?" Julian continued.

"Which question shall I answer first?" Jane replied, smiling at their consternation.

"I think it will be easier if you decide which, what and how, to start with anyway," said Caroline quickly, before Julian could reply.

Julian condescendingly nodded in agreement.

"Before I begin," said Jane, "can I say how nice it is to see you again after all these years. I should have welcomed you properly when I first spoke to you upstairs, but the surprise of seeing you both looking at that picture made me forget my manners. Please forgive me."

"Considering the way you responded to my question upstairs and your interest now, indicates to me that you can't remember many of the details and events that preceded the time you left the village, and am I correct in assuming you would like to know more about what happened?"

Jane paused slightly, as if she was waiting for a reply to her rhetorical question.

Then continued before they could answer, "One thing you should know before we go any further, is that your past is very much intertwined with the history and past events of this village. Some of the things that have happened to your family are not very pleasant and could possibly resurrect old memories, which you would prefer not to remember."

"You may also learn somethings about other members of your family best not known. Perhaps, it would be better for you to leave things as they are now and return to London, or wherever you have chosen to live. This would allow you to just recall those happy childhood memories of the village you obviously have at the moment."

"I must warn you, once I have started to tell you what I know, and you take it further, could be like opening 'Pandora's Box' and all the consequences that had. Do you still want to know?"

This time Jane waited for a reply.

Julian and Caroline looked at each other in silence for a few moments. Caroline gave a slight nod, and Julian responded with a quick smile. Then turning and looking Jane straight in the eye, replied, "That is exactly why we have returned to the village. We both want to know everything there is to know about our past; even if it's unpleasant."

"I had hoped, when you left," continued Jane, "that someday you would return to this village and say those very words. There are a lot of things, which I think, need bringing to a satisfactory conclusion. Things that only you two can do."

"What I think I'll do is this, first I'll give you some pertinent background information, then run through some of the main events, as I know them, from just before you were born, through to when you left the village. Is that alright with you?"

They both nodded in assent.

"About forty years ago, your father was promoted the position of bank manager at the bank in the High Street. However, the post of bank manager at this particular bank was a very prestigious appointment and involved much more than just managing the bank. The reasons for this are tied up with events that happened some time ago."

"At the time when private banks where allowed, the Hewett family owned our bank here, and as was usual at that time, it was handed down father to son. This continued until it was amalgamated into the larger banking concern that runs it today," Jane paused.

"You do know that your real name is Hewett, don't you?" She asked.

"Yes," replied Julian. "But it's easier for us to use these other names at the moment."

"Yes, and in the present situation, it probably is a very good idea, as you are less likely to be recognised from your physical appearance than from a well-known name. However, I digress, your great, great grandfather, I think that's the right number of great's, who was a Hewett, set up a very peculiar legacy and trust fund, although I'm not sure that's the right word, during his period as bank manager."

"He must also have had a brilliant legal mind, because when the bank was amalgamated, the lawyers working for the new bank could not break the connection between the house and this branch of the bank, or the nearest branch if they closed it."

"Mr Hewett had inherited 'Bank House' from his father, that's the house in the painting up-stairs. I won't go into the legal jargon as I'm not a lawyer and I don't understand it anyway. The result is that the post of bank manager would always be passed from father to son, even after the bank had been taken over."

"However, there are two conditions, which would terminate the legacy and trust fund. Firstly, if there failed to be a male blood descendant from Mr Hewett. Secondly, if the incumbent Mr Hewett committed suicide."

"In the event of either condition occurring, 'Bank House' must immediately be put on the market and sold within twenty-four hours to the highest bidder."

"But, if, after the house had been sold, it was established that the conditions had not really been met, i.e. if it was murder made to look like suicide, the person who had brought the house or his family, must return the house to its original owners or their descendants without recompense."

"Is this document still around?" Julian interrupted.

"Yes. Although, the original is in Somerset House, London, or wherever they keep that sort of thing now, but there is a certified copy in this museum. Would you like to see it? I warn you though, it's a very large document."

"No, I just wondered if it had been destroyed."

Jane continued, "Over the years, the position of bank manager at the village's bank became more and more integrated with the social and civic activities in the village."

"Eventually, the man who was the bank manager at this branch was looked up to in the same manner as the old Lord-of-the-Manner would have been, and similarly, unofficially of course, wielded considerable influence over everyone in the village and surrounding area. Consequently, the Hewett family became very powerful."

"Steven Henry Hewett, your grandfather on your father's side, made several enemies during the 1930's depression. He foreclosed several loans and mortgages taken out by some of the local families, which caused them considerable hardship. Many in the village felt he evicted them out of malice."

"When your grandfather subsequently died, which was before you were born, your father duly became the bank manager, in line with the rules of the legacy."

"I expect you went up to the church earlier today with the tour. And I suppose the Reverend Paul Jones described the strange death that happened in his church euphemistically known as the 'Hanging Banker'. Well unfortunately, it was your father who died."

"I knew I had heard about it before!" Julian exclaimed.

"Many in the village said he committed suicide because of the upset and unpleasantness caused by his father, your grandfather," continued Jane, ignoring Julian's interruption. "Unfortunately, the police could not prove how he died. But, because of the strong rumours of suicide going round the village at the time, the acting solicitors were forced under the terms of the legacy and trust fund, to put 'Bank House' up for sale."

"The highest bidder was a Mr Hewson, who's timely but very low bid secured the house for himself. It's interesting to note though, everyone else, apart from the acting solicitor, had forgotten about the conditions of sale until it was too late."

"That was how Mr Hewson managed to get 'Bank House' for a next-to-nothing bid. His family are still living there now."

"As a result of the sale, your mother and yourselves were evicted and went to live with your maternal grandmother. Your mother died shortly after of a broken heart. I can't remember what the doctor called it on the death certificate, but it was obvious what she died of."

"You two continued to live with your grandmother until she died. After which you were adopted by two of your uncles, and taken away from the village, until now."

Jane stopped speaking and silence descended onto the room.

"So ends the potted history of Julian and Caroline Hewett!" Julian underlined Jane's account in an acrimonies voice.

"Julian!" Caroline's voice scolded him.

"Sorry, Jane, I didn't mean to be nasty. What happened wasn't your fault."

"Would you mind telling us how you seem to know so much about our past," inquired Caroline.

"No, of course I don't mind. At the time you left the village, I felt there had been some kind of injustice, something didn't feel right. Hence, after all the fuss had died down, I started to look at various aspects of your past, to try and establish what really happened. I found some very strange and intriguing inconsistences. I haven't managed to resolve them to my own satisfaction, and they still remain a mystery to me."

In the silence that followed, they heard the Market Clock strike the half-hour.

Jane looked at her watch. "It's half past eight. If you don't go back soon, you will miss your dinner. Let me make a suggestion."

"Your stay in the village ends in the morning, and there's not much you can do at this point anyway. Think about what I have told you during the rest of the tour, or even longer. If you decide you will like to come back and stir the past up, please contact me, and I'll give you all the help I can. Here are my contact details."

Jane gave Julian a slip of paper on which she had written her name, address and telephone number.

"Do you think it's worth dragging the past up?" Caroline asked. "Would we gain anything by it?"

"I can't make that decision for you," replied Jane, "but I think the police had doubts about your father's so-called suicide. And from some of the things I've uncovered, so do I."

Jane let them out of the library and they walked slowly across to the hotel in silence.

The next morning, as the coach pulled away from the hotel, they both irresistibly looked towards the library.

In one of the upstairs windows, perhaps just as the original owner's wife would have done, they recognised Jane watching their departure.

Chapter 7

Jane woke to the noise of rain driving against her bedroom window. She pulled back the curtains and peered out into the murky greyness of the early morning. The leaden clouds were being driven across the sky by the howling wind, which also drove the rain onto the back of the cottage.

Today, she thought, *marks the end of the summer.*

She dressed, went downstairs and started preparing her breakfast, the kitchen clock showed seven forty. The outlook from the kitchen window, was of a lashing downpour, which she hoped might subside over the next three quarters of an hour or so, before she had to leave for the library.

A clatter of the letterbox announced the arrival of the morning post.

Having retrieved the one drenched letter from the doormat, she placed it on the side next to the boiler, in order to dry it out. Ink from the address had run into blue streaks, making it unreadable. Fortunately, her name, although badly smudged, was still just readable and had ensured the letter's destination would be to the correct house. Everyone in the village knew where Jane Perry lived.

The weather failed to improve during the day, with the result that when Jane arrived home at about five fifteen, she was soaked to the skin. It had taken approximately fifteen minutes to go up the Lower High Street from the library to her cottage. As she had walked home, the rain had driven into her face for the whole journey, which resulted in every item she had on was thoroughly sodden.

Having dumped her soaked clothing in the hand-basin, she ran a hot bath, squirted in a liberal amount of herbal bath oil, and then soaked herself in it, until the heat of the water had reached every chilled corner of her body.

Relaxed and recovered from the onslaught perpetrated by the elements, Jane returned to the kitchen. Heat from the boiler had made it nice and cosy and also dried out the letter, which had arrived that morning. It was now possible to open the letter, without rendering its contents unreadable, it read as follows:

Dear Jane,

We have carefully considered the implications and possible impact on our lives, of the information you gave us earlier this year, and our conclusion is to look into it further. Consequently, we would like to take up your kind offer of help, if it is still convenient.

Please, could you write and confirm that this is still all right, and if so, the best time to come and visit.

As we would need somewhere to stay during our visit, which would be somewhat open ended, would it be possible for you to arrange this?

We look forward to your reply.

Yours,
Julian and Caroline.

Jane smiled to herself after she had finished reading the letter. The problems and intrigue associated with the 'Hanging Banker' was one of her pet interests. As a result, she had collected a considerable amount of documentation about the Hewett family's past; starting with Joshua Hewett, who produced the original legacy, down to the natural death of Steven Henry Hewett.

However, apart from his birth, marriage and death certificates, for some unfathomable reason she had been unable to glean any factual information about John Henry Hewett, Julian and Caroline's father—'The Hanging Banker' himself.

To resolve the problem arising from Julian and Caroline's request for somewhere to stay, Jane picked up her address book and sat down by the telephone. She thumbed her way through her address book, until she came to Mrs Blackmore.

"I think Mr and Mrs Blackmore will be the perfect place for Julian and Caroline to stay," thought Jane to herself, "they take the occasional selected guests."

Having picked up the telephone, Jane dialled the appropriate number. "Hallo, Mrs Blackmore, this is Jane Perry…how are you? I have a favour to ask your husband and yourself…I had a brother and sister, contact me, who would like to come and stay in the village, so that they can to do some research about their family history."

"However, the process and the final outcome have a strong possibility of causing some, shall I say, interesting responses from various people in the village. Their stay would be open ended…Thank you, I will let them tell you about their quest. O' and yes, they are genuine brother and sister, even though their names differ."

Mr and Mrs Blackmore had brought the 'Old Manor House' in Love Lane, about eight years ago. During the sale of the house, there had been a dispute over the land boundaries associated with the house. The local solicitors, who were performing the conveyancing for the couple, had contacted Jane and asked her to help in tracing the land holdings and tenancies of the 'Old Manor House'.

She perceived the relevance of some old deeds and documents held in the museum, which resolved the argument in the Blackmore's favour. Hence, they were more than happy to assist with her accommodation problem.

A reply to Julian and Caroline's letter was duly drafted, outlining the arrangements and suggesting a suitable date for the start of their stay in the village.

The following morning, Jane posted the letter for Julian and Caroline at the post office, which was close to the library.

Jane then made her way into the library and set about sorting out various documents and files which were appertaining to the Hewett family in one way or another, plus those also appertaining to related events, which were held by the museum, in addition to some from her own personal collection.

A small room at the back of the museum had been set aside for use by students and others who wanted to do serious research in the library. It had been several years since anybody had used it for that purpose.

Consequently, it had become a storage area for old manuscripts, books and documents awaiting sorting and cataloguing. As Jane usually did the cataloguing, it was not questioned when she removed the existing piles of documents and books to a new storage area; and then assembled another set of records and documents in the room, ready for her forthcoming visitors.

Having walked back to her office, Jane suddenly realised how cold the research room was, even on a warm summer's day. Consequently, she started hunting for an electric fan heater, which was somewhere in the building.

"Have you seen the fan heater?" Jane called through to the leading library.

"It's here behind the counter," came the reply. "I'll come and get it."

Jane collected it and took it to the research room.

Chapter 8

"Julian! How are we going to get there? To the village I mean," asked Caroline. "As far as I can make out, there's no railway station in or even near Lower Darston."

"We could hire a car for the duration," he replied.

"It certainly would be less hassle if we had some form of independent transport, instead of having to rely on the local buses or cadging lifts from someone else."

"Ok then, I'll make some inquiries over the next week or so, and sort out the arrangements."

Not knowing what lay before them, they both felt a growing apprehension as the date of the trip grew ever closer.

At last, the Saturday of their departure arrived. The drive up to London, from the south, passed without incident. Hampton Court seemed the ideal place to stop for an early lunch, which they had in a small pub called 'The King's Arms', not far from the main gate of 'Hampton Court Palace'.

They took the A307 from there towards Kew Bridge, and picked up the North Circular, which connected theme with the A1 north, on the Old Great North Road. As mile after mile of the road slipped beneath the car, they both contemplated what the next fortnight, or so, would behold for them.

The diminishing traffic as they got further north, brought on a feeling of growing isolation from the relatively densely populated South.

It was late afternoon as they turned off the A1 onto the Lane leading to Lower Darston. In the driving seat, Julian now realised how awkward the corner at the bottom of White Swan Hill could be and understood why it had taken their coach driver considerable effort to negotiate it.

The 'Old Manor House' suddenly appeared on their right, as they drove along Love Lane and then disappeared just as quickly. Hence, having overshot the house, they had to drive up to the social housing estate a mile further on to turn round. They approached the house with a bit more caution from the other direction.

A row of trees stood between the front of the house and the road, making it virtually invisible. The gap in the foliage, through which the house had exposed itself when they passed in the other direction, opened onto a small parking area, suitable for three or four cars.

Julian reversed the car through the gap in the trees, and parked next to the large Volvo Estate car already there.

The name at the top of the address Jane had sent them, lead them to expect an old house, at least a hundred or so years old. However, as they walked towards the front door it was obvious that it had been built in the twenties or thirties, in a mock Tudor style.

When Mrs Blackmore opened the door in response to their knock, she welcomed them like long lost friends.

"Welcome, it's really nice to have you stay with us and I'm sure you will be very comfortable. Please come in, and make yourselves at home."

"Thank you," said Julian. "The name of your house led us to expect a somewhat older establishment."

"Yes I know; all our visitors think that on their first visit. The previous owners gave the house its name, but I don't know why they chose such a misleading one."

Mrs Blackmore dominated who ever she met, not because of her actions or tone of voice, but because of her sheer size. Being over six-foot-tall, and with a large sturdily built frame, she couldn't help but become the focal point of any gathering. In contrast, her voice had a soft quality about it, with a faint Yorkshire twang.

She chatted on quite happily without any prompting from Julian or Caroline, as she showed them round the house and up to their rooms.

"I thought these two rooms, next to each other at the front of the house would be most suitable, don't you?"

"Yes, I'm sure they will be," replied Caroline.

"I'll make a pot of tea, and set it in the lounge, ready for when you've unpacked."

"Thank you."

Julian arrived in the lounge first, just as Mrs Blackmore brought the tea things through.

"Here you are. There's nothing quite like a cup of tea to revive one's strength after a long journey."

"Thanks."

"Miss Perry said you are brother and sister, but I'm intrigued to know why you have different names."

"It's no secret, we were adopted when we were very young by two different families, and as we grew up we became used to using their names rather than our real one."

"I see. You know I never thought of that. I suppose it saves a lot of unnecessary explaining. Will you be staying in tonight, for dinner I mean?"

"Yes, we will. We haven't made any plans for this evening," answered Caroline, who had joined them during the conversation.

"Good, Jane asked me to give her a ring, if you were staying in for dinner, because she would like to come and join you. I hope you don't mind?"

"No. Of course we don't mind."

"Will seven o'clock be all right for you?"

"Yes, that's fine."

"I'll leave you to unwind, if there is anything you want, just shout."

Jane arrived at quarter to seven, and was ushered into the lounge. "Hallo, Julian. Hallo, Caroline. Did you both have a good drive up?"

"Hallo, Jane. Yes, we did, thanks. Although, we were surprised at how much slower the pace of life up here seems to be." The conversation among the three of them continued in a similar light-hearted manner, until Mrs Blackmore called them through to the dining room for dinner.

After they had sat down round the table, Julian asked in conversational manner, "Is there a Mr Blackmore?"

"Yes, although, I'm afraid he isn't here at the moment, he is a semi-retired barrister, and is staying in London until his current case is finished," replied Mrs Blackmore. "He should be back Tuesday or Wednesday of next week. By the way, please call me Elizabeth, Mrs Blackmore is so formal."

As the meal progressed, Jane and Elizabeth reminisced about various past happenings in the village, in a way that involved Julian and Caroline in the conversation.

"Apart from her excellent cooking, there is a reason why I thought it would be a good idea for you to stay here," Jane said to Julian and Caroline.

They had finished dinner, and the four of them were relaxing in the lounge.

"I don't know if you have been interrogated yet," Jane continued, and smiled at Elizabeth, who blushed slightly. "But Elizabeth has an extremely useful talent, which I'm sure will probably come in very handy in your task ahead. She can, as you may have experienced already, extract information from a person, simply by chatting to them."

Julian smiled to himself, as he remembered his earlier conversation and how, without thinking or hesitation, he had revealed things about his and Caroline's past he would never divulge to others. His eyes met Elizabeth's, who smiled knowingly back.

Jane laughed. "I think you will find it a very useful ability to have available during your investigation, don't you?"

"Elizabeth, do you know why we are here?" Caroline asked.

"Yes, but don't worry. Although, I may be good at extracting seemingly trivial information, I do not give any out. The true reason for you visit will not be revelled by me, you can be assured of that."

Chapter 9

"Ah, right on time," said Jane.

It was nine o'clock Monday morning, when Julian and Caroline arrived in the Library's foyer, at the same instant as Jane came out of the lending section.

"Good morning, Jane."

"I have assembled the relevant documents and other material, at least those available to me, in the research room, through here," continued Jane, opening an inconspicuous door located to one side of the main staircase.

They followed Jane down a short passage which opened out into a small anti-room with two other doors leading off it. The area had obviously been the domain of the domestic staff, during the buildings early life as a home. A long wooden board was attached to the wall above the door through which they had just emerged.

Brass plates, now tarnished almost black, were still attached along the bottom of the board, with just discernible names of the various rooms throughout the house. Above some of the brass labels, were the remains of the bells that summoned the relevant servant to his or her task.

Entering the room indicated by Jane, they found the papers she had assembled.

"These are all the documents I could find here in the library, and also some I had at home," Jane said. "I don't know if they are what you want, if not, perhaps they will contain information that could give you a lead, or point you in the right direction. I've arranged coffee, is there anything else you need."

"No, coffee will be just fine," replied Caroline.

"By the way, this room can get quite cold, even on a warm day, so I have provided a fan heater for you to use, if you feel cold."

"Thank you," Julian said.

The room, which was about ten foot square, was windowless. Drab Magnolia coloured distemper covered the walls. Although, it had obviously been decorated quite recently, which together with the single pendant light in the centre, gave the room a cell like atmosphere.

"This looks very boring," remarked Julian, after Jane had left.

"Surely, you didn't expect the information we wanted would be written in blood on the wall, did you?" Caroline retorted back.

They split the pile of papers into two smaller heaps, and taking one heap each, the task of reading through them began.

In due course, Jane arrived with coffee and after a few pleasantries left. "This reminds me of doing basic research at university," commented Julian, "that was boring too."

"Stop moaning. The sooner we get through this, the more time we'll have to ask questions and checkout other, perhaps less tedious avenues of enquiry."

Silence descended on the room again, punctuated by occasional rustling noises made as papers where moved around, or one of them made some pertinent note for future reference.

"It's one o'clock, are you two going out for lunch?" Jane called from the door at far end of the short passage.

"Yes, we are, come on, Caroline," responded Julian, leaping out of his chair. "It'll give us a break and sharpen our brains."

"I'm coming," said Caroline.

"The library closes to the public until two thirty. But if you want come back earlier, ring the top bell on the front door and I'll let you in," Jane told them as they emerged into the library's entrance area.

"Thanks," replied Caroline.

"Anne's seems as good as anywhere," Julian suggested, as they stood in the library's small forecourt.

The midday menu at Anne's seemed to be aimed at the local working community, rather than the tourist. Showing a restricted selection of robust main-courses, with simple sweets to follow, all at a very reasonable cost.

They managed to obtain a table next to the window overlooking the Square and made their selection to the waitress, who came over almost immediately.

"How are you doing with your pile of documents," Julian asked.

"Nothing of startling importance; general correspondence, and a few birth, marriage and death certificates. Mostly relevant to several generations before Mum and Dad's. How about you?"

"Very similar actually. In fact, I'm a bit disappointed. Although, I did notice that that Will or Legacy linking the bank and the house, is at the bottom of your pile. Perhaps, it will provide more meaningful information."

Lunch arrived.

"Changing the subject," said Julian, "this place is a bit schizophrenic. In the mornings and afternoons, it's geared up for the tourists, but at lunch time it only seems to cater for the locals, which is a good thing. It means that the locals have not been abandoned for to sake of the tourist trade."

"The owners, or rather the staff, seem to cope with it very well though. Perhaps it's more obvious to us as we are tourists one minute and then workers the next," noted Caroline.

They devoured their meals in a fairly relaxed manner. Sweet followed the main course, almost instantly, after which came a mug of hot coffee.

"What I didn't expect is how friendly and helpful everyone is towards us. Although, I wonder if they would be the same, if they knew what our real names are and what the real purpose for our being here is," Caroline propounded.

"That is an interesting thought. Though, Jane proposed that the result of our grandfather's actions during the depression was a level of hate for our family that hasn't yet fully subsided."

"I hope that when we have resolved the problems, we are bound to come across, some of the latent hate will become resolved at the same time."

Julian finished his coffee and looked at his watch.

"It's just before two o'clock, do you want to go back to the library, or go for a walk for half-an-hour or so?"

"I think it would be a good idea to go back to the library, and get on with going through those documents, etc."

"I agree with you; come on then, let's get back."

"Hallo, Jane," Julian said, after Jane had let them in.

"We thought the sooner we got back to them the sooner we would be finished."

"I admire your perseverance; many researchers would have finished for the day by now. I'll organise drinks for you about three-thirty, if that's alright for you? Although, if you finish before then, you know where my office is," Jane said with a big smile on her face.

"Chance, will be a fine thing," Julian retorted, and returned the big smile.

"See you later, Jane, thanks for your help," Caroline added. Both of them made their way to the research room.

"Jane is right, this room has developed a chill, please put that heater on, Julian."

"Ok."

Chapter 10

Julian and Caroline arrived back at the 'Old Manor House', at just after five o'clock.

"Would you like a cup of tea?" Mrs Blackmore asked, after she had let them in.

"Yes please," replied Caroline. "Will Jane be at dinner this evening?"

"I'll phone and ask her."

"Thank you."

Both of them sat themselves down in the lounge, and tea arrived. "I have phoned Jane and she will be coming," announced Mrs Blackmore.

"Thank you very much," responded Caroline. "By the way, would it be possible for Jane to come to dinner for the next few days as well."

"I can see no reason why not, provided she wants come that is." Jane arrived at seven forty-five, by the time she had settled down, Elizabeth called them through for dinner.

"Elizabeth said that you asked for me to be here for dinner, so am I correct in assuming you have something you want to discuss with me?" Jane asked.

"Yes," responded Caroline. "We have read most of the documentation you provided at the library, thank you for that.

Julian and I now feel we need to progress, and we wondered if you had any ideas of what we should do next. One thing I thought would be a help, is a family tree. Is there one already?"

"The short answer is no, there isn't a family tree. However, I agree with you a family tree will help to put all those births, marriages and deaths into some sort of context."

"Could I do that tomorrow at the library?" Caroline asked.

"Elizabeth, will your husband be at dinner tomorrow night?" Julian asked.

"Do not see any reason why Edward won't be."

"Jane, could I borrow the legacy document tomorrow evening, I want to ask Mr Blackmore to have a look at it. Because he has a legal mind, he may see things we have all missed."

"I can see no reason why you can't borrow the document, provided it's taken care of," replied Jane.

"Is there anything I can do to help?" Elizabeth asked.

"Yes, I think there is. Is there a place where gossip can be heard, or spread?" Julian asked.

"I'm sure I know one; Anne's, especially about ten-thirty in the morning."

"Good, would you mind going and having a coffee or something, whilst spreading it about that your two new visitors are doing a university research project about unusual deaths, and that we had heard about a death called the 'Hanging Banker' up at the church and would be very interested to hear of any details or rumours about it. And let's see what comes out of the woodwork."

"I want to look at the Electoral Register to discover who's living in Nan's old house now, and who is living in the rest of the terraced houses."

They finished dinner and moved back into the lounge, where the conversation turned to more congenial subjects.

The next day, Tuesday morning, Julian and Caroline arrived at nine o'clock sharp at the library. Jane let them in and escorted them to the reference library and the research room respectively. Around lunch time, Jane presented Julian with a large cardboard tube.

"That has got the legacy document in it, please take care of it and I'll see you at the Blackmore's this evening."

"Thank you, yes I will take great care of it," replied Julian.

Tuesday evening, after they arrived back at the 'Old Manor House', found them being introduced to Edward Blackmore.

"Julian, this is Edward, my husband, and this is Julian."

"Nice to meet you, Sir," Julian said as he shook Edward's hand.

"Please don't be so formal, Edward will do nicely."

"Thank you, Edward, and this is Caroline, my sister. Your wife will no doubt be pleased to tell you why we have different last names."

The three of them made themselves comfortable in the lounge, whilst Elizabeth made tea.

After a few moments silence, Edward commented, "According to my wife, you have something you want me to look at, Julian."

"Yes, if it's no bother?"

"No, it's no bother, in fact, judging from Elizabeth's enthusiasm, I'd be wearing my dinner, if I didn't."

Julian reaching over and removed the legacy from its tube, and gave it to Edward.

"This is a certified copy of the original document. Jane from the Library knows where the original is kept; please would you have a look at it and tell us if it's still enforceable? You may already know that part of it has already been executed. Although, we don't know yet if it will need to be enforced. But we would like to know if it legally can?"

Jane had arrived by now, as Edward started to peruse the document. "It certainly has been drafted by a very clever legal mind," Edward mumbled, to himself.

At that point, Elizabeth called them through for dinner.

"I will need to go over this very carefully. I'll do that tomorrow. But now it's dinner time," announced Edward.

Dinner progressed pleasantly accompanied by light banter.

"There are drinks in the lounge," announced Elizabeth.

"Good, I can show you the family tree I have constructed," Caroline commented.

She laid a sheet of paper out on the coffee table, and they all gathered round.

Hewett family tree.

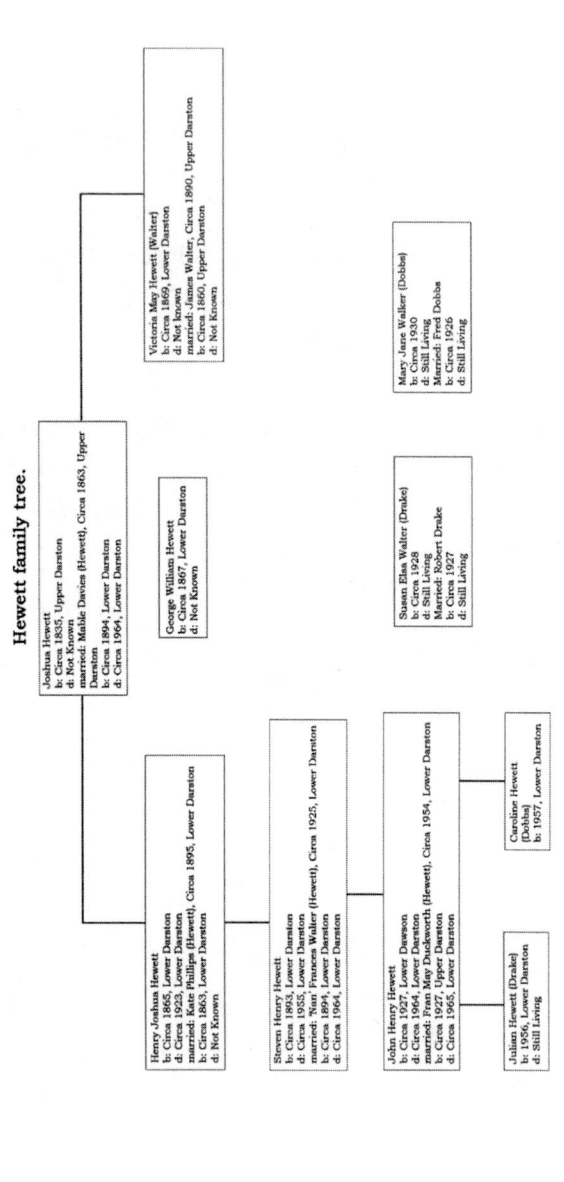

Joshua Hewett
b: Circa 1835, Upper Darston
d: Not Known
married: Mable Davies (Hewett), Circa 1863, Upper Darston
b: Circa 1894, Lower Darston
d: Circa 1964, Lower Darston

Victoria May Hewett (Walter)
b: Circa 1869, Lower Darston
d: Not Known
married: James Walter, Circa 1890, Upper Darston
b: Circa 1860, Upper Darston
d: Not Known

George William Hewett
b: Circa 1867, Lower Darston
d: Not Known

Mary Jane Walter (Dobbs)
b: Circa 1930
d: Still Living
Married: Fred Dobbs
b: Circa 1926
d: Still Living

Henry Joshua Hewett
b: Circa 1865, Lower Darston
d: Circa 1923, Lower Darston
married: Kate Phillips (Hewett), Circa 1895, Lower Darston
b: Circa 1863, Lower Darston
d: Not Known

Susan Elsa Walter (Drake)
b: Circa 1928
d: Still Living
Married: Robert Drake
b: Circa 1927
d: Still Living

Steven Henry Hewett
b: Circa 1893, Lower Darston
d: Circa 1955, Lower Darston
married: Nan Frances Walter (Hewett), Circa 1925, Lower Darston
b: Circa 1894, Lower Darston
d: Circa 1964, Lower Darston

John Henry Hewett
b: Circa 1927, Lower Dawson
d: Circa 1964, Lower Darston
married: Fran May Duckworth (Hewett), Circa 1954, Lower Darston
b: Circa 1927, Upper Darston
d: Circa 1965, Lower Darston

Caroline Hewett (Dobbs)
b: 1957, Lower Darston

Julian Hewett (Drake)
b: 1956, Lower Darston
d: Still Living

"What are the names in brackets?" Elizabeth asked.

"They are where they changed their names; like when they got married or were adopted," enlightened Julian.

"If you look at the husband of Victoria May Hewett, Joshua Hewett's daughter," said Caroline, pointing at her name on the family tree, "you can see he's a James Walker. Now, Nan and her two sisters are all Walker's as well, however, although they are of the same family, they are not on the same branch of the family. So Dad was not married to a second cousin."

"At least, we won't go ga ga then," interjected Julian.

"Another interesting point about Joshua's children," continued Caroline, scowling at Julian, "is George William Hewett. When he turned eighteen years old, he just disappeared. There is no further mention of him in any of the public records."

"For example, he is mentioned in the 1881 census as being at home at the age of fourteen. But there is no mention of him in the 1891 census, when he would have been twenty-four. Also, he's not on the 1885 nor the 1886 Electoral Registers, or any of them after that, come to that matter."

"As a result of his disappearance, Joshua, who was considerable rich at that time, disinherited him. There was also a rumour mentioned in a family letter, that George had married, however, I couldn't find any certified reference to it."

"Julian, what did you discover in the Electoral Register for 'Church Lane?'" Jane asked.

"When Steven Henry Hewett died, Nan, his wife, couldn't stay at Bank House, because John Henry, his son, and family were legally required to move in, in accordance with the legacy. So the bank brought number five Church Lane for her to live in. After Nan died, number five was sold on the open market to a Mr Robinson and his young family, who still live there now."

"With regard to number six, where the old church warden lived, it must be owned by the church, because another church warden is now living there. I assume the old church warden died. Number three, where we thought someone was watching us walk along the lane, is lived in by a Mrs Jones, who is old enough to have lived there when Nan moved in."

"I think she could be a great source of information, if we could get her in the right sort of mood. Perhaps it's someone Elizabeth could try and talk to?"

"Well," Elizabeth, chimed in, "I have sowed the seeds you suggested yesterday evening, and although nothing has arisen yet, I did notice some ears prick up. Perhaps it would be a good idea, if you, Julian and Caroline, joined Edward and myself for a coffee at Anne's, at about ten fifteen tomorrow morning."

"That sounds a great idea," announced Caroline.

Chapter 11

Julian and Caroline arrived at Anne's to find that Mr and Mrs Blackmore had already ensconced themselves at a table for four, thus, they walked over and sat in the two empty chairs.

"Welcome, to you both," said Elizabeth. "We have only just got here ourselves. Are you ready to order?"

"Yes, I am at least," replied Julian.

"So am I," responded Caroline.

"The waitress is just coming," observed Julian. "I'll get these. What would you two like?" He asked Elizabeth and Edward.

"I'll have a pot of tea and a toasted tea cake, and what about you, Edward."

"I'll have just have a coffee, with nothing to eat." "What about you, Caroline?"

"I'll have a coffee and a scone with jam and clotted cream, please." "And I'll have the same as you."

"Is there anything else?" The waitress asked. "No that's it, thank you."

"Do you think that because it's Wednesday, the same people will come in," asked Julian.

"Well it's only during the afternoon, when the shops are closed," answered Elizabeth, "so I would expect it to be the same people who come in this morning. Although, not everyone would come each day. Consequently, we should see some who were here yesterday and some new ones and some who were here yesterday will not be here today. Does that make sense?"

"I think so," Edward responded.

"Well, there at least two tables full of people from yesterday," Elizabeth noted in a low voice. "And I'm sure that little old lady, who has just came in, was here yesterday as well."

Several more individuals and groups came in, until Anne's was almost full up. The four of them chatted about this and that for about half an hour. Having finished their food and drinks, they started to think about leaving.

Before they could move, the little old lady got out of her chair and walked over to Elizabeth and handed her a letter. "I think this letter is for you," she said handing it to Elizabeth.

"O' thank you. Yes, it's got my address on it. Thank you so much."

The little old lady acknowledged Elizabeth's thank you and left the café. "Well, I've got to get back home, that's if you want a sensible answer about that document," commented Edward.

"I'll come with you," said Elizabeth. "What are you two going to do?"

"I think we shall go over to the library for an hour or so, then come back here for some lunch. After which, we shall probably make our way back to the house sometime this afternoon, if that's alright by you," mooted Caroline.

"That's perfectly fine."

They all left Anne's, and Julian and Caroline headed for the library, whilst Mr and Mrs Blackmore started down the Lower High Street.

"I fancy an iced bun from the cake shop before we go in," Caroline suggested.

"That is a good suggestion," retorted Julian. "As I brought the coffees, you can get the iced buns."

Caroline disappeared into the cake shop. Reappearing, after a few moments, with two iced buns.

"To the base of the clock tower," commanded Julian. Having finished their buns, they headed to the library.

"What do you intend doing?" Caroline asked.

"Well, I've got numbers one, two, and four Church Lane to investigate. What about you?"

"I'm going to see if I can find anything more about our disappeared George. He can't have fallen of the planet and there is always some kind of paper trail."

By this time, they were in the entrance foyer of the library. "See you down here about one o'clock."

Then they both went off to their different rooms.

Caroline arrived in the foyer just before one o'clock, surprised to find Julian already there, talking to Jane.

"You realise the library is not open this afternoon, I was just telling Julian."

"Yes, I guessed it might not be. Anyway, we will see you tonight."

They all left the library. Jane turned right towards her home and Julian and Caroline crossed over and entered Anne's.

Their lunch arrived promptly.

"I posted a letter to Veronica this morning," mentioned Caroline as they were eating. "As she is a genealogist, I thought she might be able to throw some light on George's disappearance. The woman in the post office seemed to be as grumpy as the first day she spoke to me."

"Blamed all the tourists for spoiling the village. I thought I did well for not having a go at her."

"Well done for that, anyway. What did you send Veronica?"

"A copy of his birth certificate and a copy of the two census'."

Having finished lunch, they started to dawdle down Lower High Street towards Love Lane and 'the Manor House'. Julian let both of them into the house with the key they had been given, and they then made themselves comfortable in the lounge.

"How did you get on with Church Lane?" Caroline inquired.

As she asked the question, Elizabeth came in and asked, "Would you like a cup of tea or coffee?"

"Tea please," responded Caroline.

"Same for me, please," said Julian. "There isn't much to comment about. Numbers four and two were relatively new to the area. Number one was occupied by a middle-aged couple, Mr and Mrs Samuels, but I couldn't work out how long they had lived at number one. Perhaps Jane will know."

Elizabeth had returned with the tea, and sat down with them.

"Can I be nosy?" Julian asked. "And inquire what was in your letter from the little old lady?"

"Well, it's actually addressed to you two. She said if you would like to go round to her house, number three Church Lane, she has some information you might find interesting. She suggested I might like to come along as well."

"Wow, I didn't expect a response that quickly. So it was her who watched us from her window, when we first visited the village on the coach. Do you think she recognised us?"

A short while later, Jane arrived.

"Jane, would you like some tea?" Elizabeth asked. "Do you two want a refill? That pot must be cold by now."

They all nodded in assent.

"Jane, what do you know about the woman who runs the post office?" Caroline asked.

"Well, she lives by herself on the social housing estate, which is a bit further up this road. She started working in the post office as an assistant about fifteen years ago, and took over running it a few years later after the old postmistress died. She has a small circle of friends, but I'm not one of them and the majority of the villagers keep her at arm's length."

"There is an old rumour, which I don't know if there is any truth in it or not, that she had an affair about thirty years ago."

"Do you know who with?" Julian asked.

"It was supposed to have been with a Mr Hewson, the same one as brought 'Bank House', but he got shot of her as soon as he got hold of the house deeds. Whether the two events are connected, I don't know."

"That seems a bit fishy," observed Caroline.

Edward had arrived whilst the discussion was going on. "Would you like to hear about your document?" Edward asked.

"Yes, please," Julian and Caroline responded together.

"From a legal point of view, yes, it is still active. However, the only part that is viable is if you can prove, without doubt, that your father was murdered and did not commit suicide. In that case, you would be able to reclaim possession of the house."

"But, it could turn into quit a legal battle. Basically, you would need to have your father's current death certificate overturned and have a new one with the words 'Was Murdered by person or persons unknown' entered, or words to that effect."

"It would defiantly need the words 'Was Murdered' inserted, which would mean proving the police got it wrong at the original inquest, and that will be extremely hard."

"Thank you very much for all your effort, Edward," said Julian.

"Actually, I found it stimulating to have something with an unusual legal argument to look at."

"Can I impose something else on you?" Julian inquired.

"It depends on what it is, you'll need to ask me before I agree."

"Yes, of course. Would it be possible to get a look at the files the police have on our father's death?"

"I'll need to make a few inquiries before I can answer that question. I will get back to you as soon as possible."

"Thank you."

Silence descended for the moment or two, until Elizabeth announced dinner was ready.

Having finished their meal and retired to the lounge.

Elizabeth asked, "What shall we do about Mrs Jones tomorrow?"

"Well, it was about ten thirty yesterday, when she came into Anne's. So I would suggest we walked over to her house between nine o'clock and nine thirty. What do you think, Caroline?"

"That sounds fine by me."

"I'll get breakfast ready for seven thirty then, any objections?"

"Yes, I do," Edward mumbled.

"Well that is just tough," responded Elizabeth.

"I thought it might be," Edward replied.

The three of them left the 'Old Manor house' just before nine o'clock the next morning, and arrived at Mrs Jones house about nine fifteen.

"Please come in, Mrs Blackmore, and your two visitors." Mrs Jones showed them into the parlour.

"Please make yourselves comfortable, whilst I go and make some tea. The kettle has just boiled." A few moments later, Mrs Jones returned with a tray. She poured four cups of tea. "There we are, help yourselves to milk and sugar."

"Let me introduce these two, this is Julian Drake and this Caroline Dobson," announced Mrs Blackmore, "and please call me Elizabeth."

"So you two have taken the names of your adopters, I recognised you, when you came to visit the village the other week on the coach, as Julian and Caroline Hewett."

"You must have a very good memory," remarked Julian.

"Well, I should remember you both, the number of times you came round here to play, when your Nan had to go out for some reason or other."

"I thought I recognised the house when we came in," commented Caroline. "Does that mean that you are Auntie 'Lily'?"

"Yes, that is what you used to call me. My name is Lily Jones."

"Well, that is a turn up for the books," commented Julian. "I'm sorry we didn't recognise you."

"I'm not surprised that you had forgotten me, considering the trauma you were put through around the time your Nan died."

"Please can we ask you not to spread it about, as to whom we really are?" Julian asked.

"I can understand why you would not want that, and I will keep it confidential. I also realise why you are interested in the events leading to and around the death of your father."

Chapter 12

"Lily, in your letter you stated that you had some information that we might find interesting," inquired Elizabeth.

"Well, I think you may find it interesting. I moved into this house when Steven Henry Hewett was bank manager and living in Bank House, which was about 1950. He was promoted to bank manager when his father, Henry Joshua, died in 1923, which meant Steven Henry was bank manager during the great depression of the late twenties and early thirties."

"Unfortunately, a considerable number of companies and private people for that matter, had loans and mortgages with the bank, which was forced to foreclose on them. Unfortunately, it caused considerable hardship for several families in and around the village."

"Also, about that time, the bank was taken over by one of the big four banks, the one that still runs it now. However, your Nan told me that under the management of Steven Henry, the bank's capital had dwindled to a level where the bank would have become bankrupt over the next couple of years, at the most."

"As you probably know, the great depression did not only affect this village, but also every village, town and country thought the world were affected in some way or another."

"Lawyers from the new bank tried very hard to break the connection between the Hewitt family, the 'Bank House' and the bank's managerial position, but failed to find a legal way of doing it."

"Although, the lawyers did find a way of controlling the bank's finances, by installing a financial manager, who answered directly to the bank's head office. Thereby, making the bank manager's situation almost a purely ceremonial position."

"Nonetheless, during the period between the take over and Steven's death in 1955, Steven had managed to arrange some monetary transactions with at least one family, probably more, which the bank's financial manager didn't know about, but they did come to light, when an audit was conducted just after your father took up the position of manager."

"After the audit, a couple of families were taken to court and charged with fraud, which resulted in all their assets being confiscated. This episode left a huge stain on the Hewitt family name, and your father was lumbered with resolving the situation."

"However, instead of working against the financial manager as Steven did, your father decided to work with him. From what your Nan told me, they seemed to get on well together."

"Sorry to interrupt, but do you know the name of the financial manager?" Julian asked.

"No, I'm afraid I can't remember. However, he wasn't very old when he took up the post, so there is a possibility that he is still working for them, or at least he could be still alive. Perhaps, the bank will be able to help you."

"It took three to four years before your father and the financial manager eventually got the bank's finances back in order. After that, according to your Nan, things seemed too settle down for the final five years of your father's life."

"Although, there is one thing I remember your Nan telling me, which seemed strange when you look at it in hindsight, which was that your father became ill during the last fortnight of his life. It wasn't a debilitating illness, more like a bad cold or a mild case of flu that came on slowly. In fact, he still went to work each day as normal. Whether it's relevant, I don't know."

"What day did he die on?" Caroline asked.

"It was a Tuesday morning, about ten o'clock, when one of the usual cleaners found him and called the Vicar. However, as he was already dead when they found him. He must have died sometime earlier."

"Was the Vicar the reverend Paul Jones?"

"Yes, he had just taken up the position about six months before."

"You have been very helpful, Mrs Jones," commented Julian. "By the way, am I correct in assuming you are not related to Paul Jones?"

"Yes, you are correct. No, I'm not related to Paul Jones. If I remember anything else, I'll be in touch."

"Thank you so much, you have been very helpful and thank you for the tea."

Mrs Jones showed them to the door and let them out.

They walked back to the 'Old Manor House'. It was nearly half past twelve by the time they had settled themselves in the lounge.

"I'm not expecting Edward back yet a while, and as it's a bit late to get to Anne's for lunch, would you like a sandwich to see you through to this evening?"

"Yes please," replied Caroline. Julian nodded in agreement.

"Ham or Cheese?"

"Ham will be just fine, thank you."

In due course, a tray arrived with two plates of sandwiches and a pot of tea and three cups; there was also a plate with some jam tarts on it.

"Well, what do you think of this morning's revelations?" Elizabeth asked.

"It was nice to hear an account about our family, without any prejudice, well as far as I could tell, anyway." responded Caroline.

"It has at least given us some new leads to follow," chimed in Julian. "We have the reverend Paul Jones, who may have something he has kept to himself all this time, which could be relevant."

"We also have the bank and whoever the financial manager was at that time. Perhaps, Jane will be able to remember the name of the bank manager who took over from Dad?"

"If Edward has any luck with the police at Grantham, we may have some records to go through relating to Dad's actual death."

"Although, it's probably not relevant, Dad's illness during the last two weeks of his life is particularly intriguing."

"It also looks like a large number of people and families were upset by the actions of Steven Henry. I wonder who and by how much?"

"O' I almost forgot, George William Hewett, he is a bit of a mystery. Maybe he's got nothing to do with Dad's death. Although, if he got jealous of Steven Henry inheriting all that wealth and him getting absolutely nothing, may have laid seeds for some kind of revenge."

"Elizabeth, what do you think?"

"Well, I had the distinct impression the Mrs Jones knows a lot more than she has told us so far. It may have been so as not to upset you, but I think there something very relevant to be revealed in due course. Don't worry, I'll eventually discover what it is over the next few days or so."

"Anyway, you must excuse me, as I have to start dinner." Shortly after, Mr Blackmore returned home.

"Hello, you two," Edward said, as he walked into the lounge. "Have you had a good day?"

"An interesting one," replied Caroline. At that point, Jane came in to join them.

"What was so interesting, then?" Jane asked.

"We'll tell you about it over dinner when we are all together." It wasn't long before Elizabeth called them through for dinner.

Caroline opened the conversation. "Mrs Jones remembered things first hand from about 1950, which is when she moved on to number three Church Lane. Our Nan moved into Number five sometime during 1955. Apparently, Steven Henry upset a number families and individuals during the great depression of the 1920s and 30s, by calling in a number bank loans and mortgages."

"Another interesting fact is that the bank was nearly made bankrupt by Steven Henry, which resulted in the bank installing a financial manager, who was responsible for all monetary transactions. However, Steven still managed make some transactions without the financial manager's knowledge."

"Mrs Jones thought the financial manager was still working at the bank, or at least still alive. Jane, do you remember the name of the financial manager in the late 1950's?"

"No, but I know there is a record of it at the library. I'll get it tomorrow."

"Mrs Jones also said that our father became ill during the fortnight before he died, apparently it wasn't that bad because he still went to work."

Edward suddenly commented, "Now that is interesting! Did she give any information as to what the illness was?"

"No, she thought it was just a bad cold, or perhaps a mild attack of flu."

"By the way, I had a long conversation with the chief constable over lunch today, concerning the possibility of you being able to go through the police archives relating to your father's death. He was of the opinion, there is no objection in principal. However, he would need to check because it was a local case, and there may be a local objection from the officers who were involved."

"Particularly, if they thought they could be subjected to judicial proceedings over the possibility of a miscarriage of justice being uncovered. He is going to get back to me some time tomorrow. The archives themselves are located in Grantham."

"There is still hope then that we will be able to go through them then," responded Julian.

"Yes, quite a good chance actually."

"We also found out that George William Hewett, Henry Joshua Hewett's brother, disappeared when he turned about eighteen years of age, and hasn't been heard of since. I have written to my friend, Veronica, who is a genealogist, regarding George's disappearance, in the hope she can find out where he is, or was, as he would be well over one hundred years old now."

"Right," said Julian. "To summarise what we are going to pursue from tomorrow?"

"There is: the Reverend Paul Jones, the bank's financial manager, The police archives, and perhaps later, the mystery concerning George."

"Jane, would it be alright if Caroline and I call in on you at the library first thing in the morning to get the name of the bank's financial manager. We can then go over to the bank and try to get an appointment with him."

"Leave Lily Jones to me," volunteered Elizabeth. "Although, it may take a couple of days or so, to find out what secrets she is hiding."

"That's fine by us, thank you very much for offering."

"If we don't get an interview at the bank tomorrow, we'll go and see if we can talk with Reverend Paul Jones."

"If that's everything," commented Elizabeth, "let us into the lounge."

"Hang on a minute," Caroline suddenly interjected. "What about Mr Hewson, who bought Bank House after Dad supposedly committed suicide? Is he still alive? I assume his family are still living at Bank House. He also had an affair with that post office woman."

"I'll check the Electoral Register at the library tomorrow as well," said Jane. "He could have something interesting to say, or just tell us to get lost."

"From our visit to the post office, during our first visit to the village, the post office woman is a very short tempered and cantankerous person," recounted Julian. "So I don't think I would like to interview her, unless we have no other option. By the way, what happened to her after her affair with Mr Hewson?"

"I'm not certain, the rumour is that she was divorced by her husband, which was quite an acrimonies and public battle, by all accounts. As you two were long gone from the village by then, I don't think it will have any bearing on your father's death," related Jane.

"However, as it was Mr Hewson who was involved in the divorce, I wouldn't be at all surprised."

"One of the things, working on your father's death has taught me, is that there are a lot of people who seem have got their finger's in this case, one way or another, some of which you wouldn't expect."

Chapter 13

It was ten past nine when Julian and Caroline arrived at the library.

They went into the lending section of the library and asked for Miss Perry. After a few moments, she arrived and took them through to her office.

"I have managed to find the bank's financial manager's name, but I don't know if he is still working at this branch."

"That's not a problem, as the bank will let us know where he is," said Julian.

"The name he uses, or did use, is Jerry Cole; however, I think his real name is Jeremiah Cole. I'm sure he uses Jerry, as it doesn't sound so Jewish, but I may be wrong."

"Thanks for your help, Jane."

They left the library and headed for the bank, which was about five or ten minutes' walk away. They entered the bank and went up to the information desk.

"Please could we see Jerry Cole?" Julian asked.

"What is it in connection with?" The woman behind the desk asked.

"I'm afraid it's a private matter," answered Julian.

"Could I have your name please?"

"Julian Drake and Caroline Dobbs."

"Thank you, I'll go and see if he is available."

After a few moments, she returned. "He will be about five minutes. Would you like to wait or come back?"

"We'll wait, if that's ok."

"There are some chairs over by the wall."

"Thank you."

They seated themselves down for the wait. Ten minutes passed.

"Mr Cole will see you now," called a voice, from the door at the end of the counter.

They followed the voice through the door who then opened an inner door with 'Manager' blazoned on it.

"Mr Drake and Ms Dobbs," she announced, then stood back to let them enter.

"Please come in and have a seat," invited Mr Cole, in slightly pompous voice.

As Julian and Caroline took the indicated chairs, they noted Mr Cole looked older than they had expected. He was a rotund man, bald with a ruddy face.

"Now how can I help you?" He asked.

"We are involved in a university project examining unusual deaths," commenced Julian. "Some information we have been given indicates you were the financial manager at this bank when Mr John Henry Hewett mysteriously died in 1964 whilst he was working as manager at this bank."

"We were wondering if you could remember, or have some archives, which would give us some insight as to what happened in the lead up to his death. Even what caused his death?"

"Well, I wasn't expecting that, when I came in this morning," in a slightly less pompous voice than before. "Well it will take a couple of days to look out the archive documents, as our archivist only comes in two days a week. I suggest that you come in on Monday morning of next week, and I'll make sure they are ready for you to look at them."

"As for what I can remember myself, is a bit on the vague side. It was in the early 1950s that the bank posted me to this branch as financial manager. Steven Henry Hewett was the bank manager then. Unfortunately, what with the global depression and some mismanagement, the bank was on its last legs financially."

"Shortly after I took over the financial side of things, Steven died. After that, Steven's son, John Henry, came on board as manager. Actually, John and I worked very well together and after five or six years we managed to get the bank's finances back to a stable situation. A few years after that John died."

"We heard John was found dead up at the church. Do you know how that happened?" Julian asked.

"Not very well, two or three weeks before his death he seemed to be suffering from a cold or flu like aliment, however, he had become very paranoiac about all the hardships his father had caused during the depression of the thirties."

"Although, he still continued to come into work, even after I told him to have some time off. Then, suddenly he was discovered dead during 1954 on a Tuesday morning at the church."

"Apparently, he was hanging from one of the bell ropes. And that is about all I can remember."

"Thank you very much for your time and helping us. We will be back on Monday morning to look at the archive material."

Julian and Caroline rose to leave and Jerry came round and shook their hands.

"We open at nine fifteen and I look forward to seeing you then." They left the bank and walked back towards their lodgings.

Caroline suddenly stopped, and said, "It's half past eleven, let's go to Anne's and have some lunch, and then go and tackle Paul Jones."

"That is a good idea," responded Julian.

So they did an about turn and headed towards Anne's.

After ordering their food, Julian observed, "Jerry seemed to have his response off pat, almost as if he had learnt a prepared script. What did you think?"

"He rattled off things I wouldn't think you could remember, after twenty-five years or so. I tell you what I did notice though, that he looked very much like you."

"Do you really think so?"

"Yes, in fact, apart from his voice, he could be a stand in for you." They finished their meal, and left Anne's.

"Do you want to get the car; it looks like rain?"

"Yes."

Having picked their car up, they drove to the Vicarage; seeing the lane was a bit too narrow to park outside, they parked in the church carpark.

"Let's see if Paul's in the church," commented Julian.

Finding the church and Vestry empty, they went over to the Vicarage and knocked on the door.

After a minute or so, a woman opened the door. "Can I help you?"

"Please could we speak to the reverend Paul Jones," asked Caroline.

"Who shall say wants to see him."

"Julian Drake and Caroline Dobbs."

"Just a moment please," the woman said and then disappeared, assumable to ask if he was available.

A few moments later, she returned and asked them to follow her. She opened a door and bid them enter.

"Welcome, Julian and Caroline, to my office come library," announced, the reverend Paul Jones. "How can I be of assistance? Am I correct in assuming it's a marriage you're inquiring about?"

"No, I'm afraid not," Julian announced, "as we are actually brother and sister. It will take too long to explain why we have different names. We are here to look into the death of John Henry Hewett, as we are currently working on a university project regarding strange deaths. Death by supposedly hanging from a bell rope is certainly strange."

"I see; how can I help?"

"We've learnt that you had taken office at the church some six months before he died, and you were one of the first on the scene. We wondered what you could tell us about what you saw."

"Well, I wasn't the first one on the scene, one of the church cleaners was. But, as soon as she found him, she immediately called me. I was in the Vestry at the time when I arrived where she had found him lying on the belfry floor, with a bell rope untied and hanging just above his head."

"His face was white and felt cold to the touch. Immediately, I phoned the police."

"Was he actually hanging from the rope?" Caroline asked.

"Not when I got there. Whether the police asked the cleaner who found him the same question, I do not know."

"Once the police had arrived, I left them too it. That unfortunately, is about all I can remember."

"Do you know what the name of the cleaner was?" Julian asked. "Also, is she still alive?"

"As to whether she is still alive, I think she is. But, I cannot remember her name."

"It was just a thought. If you remember anything else, could you let us know? At the moment we are staying at the 'Old Manor House', which is in Love Lane."

"Yes, of course I will, I hope I have given you some information that will help with your research."

"We would like to thank you for all your help, which has been of great help."

Paul showed them to the front door and shook hands as Julian and Caroline left. They walked across to their car in the church carpark.

"What did you think of his response?" Julian asked Caroline, after they had settled themselves in the car.

"One interesting point he made was that when Paul first saw Dad, he was lying on the floor already cold. If Dad had been hanging from the bell rope, I don't think the cleaner would have untied him and laid him on the floor, before going to get Paul."

"In fact, if he had been hanging from the rope, it would have left a deep mark round his neck, and I'm sure Paul would have noticed it if it had been there."

"That's what I thought was strange, which raises the question: why was it assumed that he killed himself by hanging with the bell rope, and then referring to it as the 'Hanging Banker'."

"Exactly, which seems to indicate that there has been something more than meets the eye associated with Dad's death."

"Do you want to go back to the 'Old Manor House' or what?" Julian mooted.

"Well as today is Friday, it means that tomorrow and the next day are Saturday and Sunday. What are you suggesting we do on those two days?"

"On Saturday, I thought we could go and have a look round Upper Darston, and on Sunday, we could go for a walk up the river, like we did when we were small. How does that sound?"

"Yes, that sounds fine. Although, Elizabeth and Edward may have some suggestions, I think they are a very nice couple."

"Back to 'The Manor House' it is then!"

Having started the car's engine, Julian checked it was clear to pull away, when he noticed Paul Jones open his garage and ride away on a bicycle.

"I wonder where he's going." Julian inquired.

"How should I know," responded Caroline. "Quick follow him and see where he goes."

Julian shot out of the carpark, just in time to see Paul Jones dive down the alley at the rear of the terraced houses, where Lily Jones lived.

"Now why is he going down there? When I said to her on Tuesday, I assume you and Paul weren't related, she said she wasn't. But what if her dead husband was?"

"That puts a different complexion on things, if he is going to see Lily, Paul will know who we really are. I hope Elizabeth has managed to find something out about her."

Chapter 14

When Julian and Caroline arrived back at the 'Old Manner House', they found Elizabeth sitting in the lounge.

"Would you two like a cup of coffee or tea, perhaps something stronger?" Elizabeth asked.

"Would it be too presumptuous to ask for a whiskey?" Julian replied. "It's been a very bewildering day. We now have more new questions than answers."

"Let me get your whiskey first. Caroline, what would you like?"

"I'm ok, thank you."

It took Elizabeth a few moments to get Julian's whiskey. "Do you want anything in it, Julian?"

"No, thank you."

"Right, there you are. Now tell me about your bewildering day."

"Well, first we went to see Jerry Cole, who is the bank manager; he confirmed he was the financial manager when Dad died. What he told us sounded as if he had read it from a script. He said that Dad had committed suicide and been found hanging from a bell rope, up at the church. Also he said that Dad had some kind of flu like ailment during the last two or three weeks of his life."

"However, he did say that we can have a look at the bank's archive material, they have for that period, on this coming Monday. By the way, he looked a lot like Julian," Caroline added, with big grin on her face.

After taking a sip of his whisky, Julian continued, "After lunch we went to see the reverend Paul Jones. Who thought we wanted to get married? But after we explained we wanted information about Dad's death, although we didn't tell him he was our father, he came up with a couple of interesting points."

"Firstly, it was a cleaner who found him lying on the floor with the bell rope hanging over him, not round his neck. Apparently, she immediately went and found Paul Jones, who called the police. Paul said he saw the body lying on the floor; again, the bell rope was hanging over him, but not round his neck."

"Could the cleaner have untied the bell rope?" Elizabeth asked.

"We asked that question and Paul didn't think she had the time to untie him. After we had left the vicarage, we sat in the car for few moments which was parked in the church car park rather that outside the vicarage. When Paul came out, took his bike out of garage and raced off down the road."

"We followed him and were just in time to see him go down the alley behind the terraced houses where Mrs Jones lives. Although, we didn't see him go into number three, we did immediately assume that they were related in some way, despite her denial when we were with her."

"That is all very interesting," commented Elizabeth. "So we now have: Jerry Cole saying it was suicide; Paul Jones saying he wasn't hanging on the bell rope, when he was found and Mrs Jones saying nothing, either way."

"I wonder why the police decided it was suicide," questioned Caroline.

"We won't know that until we get to see the police records," replied Elizabeth. "I better start doing dinner. By the way, Jane will not be coming to dinner this evening."

"We were thinking of going to Upper Darston tomorrow, would that alright?"

"Yes, of course it is. Do you want an early breakfast and will you be back for dinner?"

"No, we don't need an early breakfast and yes, we will be back for dinner."

The next morning, while they were sitting around the dining table having breakfast, Julian suddenly blurted out, "That assumption we made yesterday about Paul Jones, could be completely wrong. We assumed the Paul Jones was going to see Mrs Jones when he went down the alley behind the terraced houses."

"But he could just a likely have been going to visit whoever is living at number four, because the church warden lives there."

"I never considered that," concurred Caroline.

"That is quite a possibility," agreed Elizabeth. "I must apologise for Edward not being back for dinner last night, but he had to go to London late yesterday morning and decided to stay over. He should be back sometime today. I hope you have a nice day in Upper Darston."

"Thanks, we'll be back for dinner."

Julian and Caroline left the house and settled themselves in their car. "Caroline, before we go to Upper Darston, I want see what the social housing estate is like. Is that ok with you?"

"I'm happy to do that. As if I dare to say otherwise," Caroline grinned at him.

Julian pulled out and turned right along Love Lane towards the housing estate. When they arrived at the roundabout, which they had driven all the way round on the day of their arrival at the 'Old Manor House', there was a choice of two ways, left or straight on.

"Go straight on," suggested Caroline.

As they drove along, they noticed that although there was a verity of styles, they were all of the typical 1940s post WWII kind with fairly wide spacing. They eventually reach what looked like the far end of the estate. The road turned left and eventually took them back to the first roundabout. Julian turned right back past the 'Old Manor House'.

"The estate seemed nice and tidy," commented Julian.

"A lot better than and certainly not as rough as some I have seen," responded Caroline.

Julian had now reached the Lower High Street; he turned left, passed over the river bridge towards Upper Darston. They passed the school on their right and suddenly they were in open country side. Ten minutes later, they came to the outskirts of Upper Darston.

"It's certainly not a village in size, more of a town," observed Caroline.

"Not a very small one at that," agreed Julian. "I wonder what the parking is like?"

"Perhaps there will be a carpark signposted in the town centre."

"We could always park in that supermarket, its carpark looks quite empty, and the entrance is on the right over there."

"Ok, in we go then. It looks like it's free."

Julian parked the car, not too close to the supermarket building. "Which way do you want to go?" Julian asked, as they stood at the entrance to the carpark. "Left is the way we came in."

"Let's turn right then," Caroline replied.

The pair of them dawdled along Upper Darston High Street.

"At least, there are more shops here than in Lower Darston," commented Caroline.

"Well, there's a café. Shall we go in?" Julian asked. "If you want to."

They entered the café and managed to find a seat by the window. They ordered their drinks and cakes and sat looking up and down the High Street.

"There's a book shop over there." Julian pointed some way down the street. "I wonder if they have book called the history of Lower Darston, or something like it."

"Well, we'd better go and find out when we've finished here." It was half an hour later, when they entered the book shop.

"This looks promising," said Julian. "Although it's got new books at the front of the shop, there are acres of older books towards the back."

"I hope they have a historic section," Caroline mused. "Perhaps even a local history section."

They wandered around several allies of book shelves, found themselves side-tracked by several unrelated but interesting looking covers, but still no local history section.

"I think I'll go and ask," Julian said with a smile.

Julian found his way back to the front of the shop, where a man was sitting behind a desk, who he assumed was the proprietor. "Excuse me, but do you have a local history section?"

"Not exactly, what is it you are looking for, because you are not from round here, are you?"

"No, we are holidaying in Lower Darston. We wondered if you had a book entitled 'The History of Lower Darston', or something along those lines?"

"There are some books of that ilk. I think it will be easier if I show you where they are, follow me."

Julian followed the proprietor towards the back of the shop, they collected Caroline along the way.

"They are located on the first floor," he said as he opened a door that lead to a flight of stairs. "The local history books are on the two sets of shelves next to the front window."

"Thanks very much for your help."

They climbed the narrow stairs and went into what was once the front bedroom, when the shop was a house, on arriving at the window they saw there was book case, attached to the wall each side of the window.

"Which one do you want look through?" Julian asked.

"That one." Caroline pointed at the on the left.

"There are several books on the Roman Occupation in the area," said Caroline.

"I've got some on the Neolithic Encampments," replied Julian. "Hang on, here's one 'Strange Happenings in the Darston Villages'."

Julian took it off the shelf and turned to the index at the back. "Well, Dad has got an entry in the index, let's see what it says." It took several moments to find the entry.

"The entry covers about fifteen pages. So it may be worth getting. The price inside the cover is eight pounds, I think I'll buy it."

They spent another ten minutes looking and then returned down stairs to pay for the book.

"You managed to find one then," commented the proprietor. "That's eight pound please."

Julian handed the money over.

"Are you interested in the history of the area then?"

"Actually, Lower Darston in particular."

"Why is that?"

"We are doing a project about a death up at the St John the Baptist church."

"The 'Hanging Banker'?"

"Yes, that's right, do you know anything about it?"

"Well, yes. It just happens, that I have written a monograph about that particular death. If you would like a copy, it's only a fiver."

"Yes, please."

The proprietor disappeared out the back of the shop and returned a few moments later with an A5 size booklet. He handed it to Julian.

"Here's your fiver. I see your name is Mr Samuels."

"Yes, that's right."

"Do you by any chance live at number one Church Lane, Lower Darston?" "Yes I do, and I'm impressed that you have found that out. You have been doing some research."

"We were looking for those who were living close to where the murder took place, so that we could interview them about it. We didn't think you were living at number one at the time of the murder. Is our assumption wrong?"

"No, you were right. We moved into number one about three years after the event. Wednesday is early closing, if you want to come round to number one in the afternoon, you will be most welcome. Here's my card, it's got my phone number and e-mail on it. Anyway, it has been a great pleasure meeting you both and I hope to see you soon."

"Thanks for your help."

They both left the shop and started walking back to the car. "That was interesting," commented Caroline.

"It certainly was, but I wonder what he really knows. Did you notice when I called it a murder, he didn't correct me and say it was suicide. I'm looking forward to reading these two books."

"Look there's a chip shop over there, shall we get some chips to eat in the car, before we go back to the 'Manor House'?"

"That is a very good idea."

They purchased their chips and settled themselves in the car.

"I noticed a layby just outside the town. That will be a much better place to eat than in a supermarket carpark."

"Come on then."

They shot out of the carpark, and within minutes they were parked in the layby overlooking the fields.

"That's much better, now where are those chips?"

Chapter 15

Having finished dinner, the four of them were drinking in the lounge.

"I have managed to arrange an appointment to see the police files relating to your father's murder, for Tuesday," Edward announced. "But, they insist that I am there with you all the time. So if we leave about eight o'clock, we'll get there about eight forty-five or there abouts. We'll go in my car, if it's all right with you?"

We both agreed with the suggestion.

"Did the two books you were reading earlier provide any new information?" Elizabeth asked.

"The 'Strange Happenings in the Darston Villages' book had a lot of detail about how it shocked the village and general back ground information."

"However, it did call the actual death a suicide. Although, the general tone of the article implied to me that it was generally a regurgitation of the gossip, which would have been circulating at the time, so there was nothing we didn't really know already," Julian commented.

"Although, the monograph produced by Mr Samuels seems to have been researched quite thoroughly," Caroline added. "Unfortunately, he doesn't mention names, I assume out of fear of being sued for libel. However, he does call it a murder."

"There was one interesting comment he made which was that the local police constable arrived very quickly after the body had been found, five or ten minutes before the main team of the police arrived. Interestingly, written in the margin in pencil against the line where the local policeman was mentioned, was the number 287. It raised the question in my mind, was that number the policeman's number?"

"We can confirm that when we go through the police records on Tuesday," added Edward.

"Are you going to do anything special tomorrow morning?" Elizabeth asked.

"We thought we would go and have a nostalgic wander along the river bank," answered Julian.

"Well, we are going to have a roast dinner about one thirty tomorrow and you both would be most welcome to join us," said Elizabeth.

"We both shall look forward to it," replied Caroline.

The next day, after a leisurely breakfast, Julian and Caroline dawdled their way towards the river.

Eventually, they arrived at the gate leading down to the river bank. "There you are," said Julian opening the gate. "Mind how you go down those steps, they look like no one has been down them for some time, and are now rather overgrown."

Julian closed the gate and followed Caroline down the steps. When Julian had joined Caroline, she got hold of his shoulders and turned him round to face the bridge. "Look at that!" She said, pointing to the arch leading underneath the bridge. It not only arched over the river, but also over the path on which they were standing.

"That must lead all the way to the other side of the bridge," stated Julian. "Come on, let see where it comes out?"

They walked along the path under the bridge, which was amply big enough for them to walk through without stooping, in fact, big enough for a Shire-horse to walk through.

After a few moments, they emerged on the other side of the road. "I think," commented Julian, "at one time barges used this river to transport cargo up and down it and this must have been the tow-path where the horses walked along pulling the barges." Julian paused for a moment and then added, "I wonder where they went?"

After a few moments pondering, Julian suggested, "Come on, let's go back through under the bridge and continue along the tow-path towards 'Bank House'."

They dawdled past the rear fences of the six terraced houses, each in various states of repair. In the distance, they could see 'Bank House'. After five or so minutes, they arrived at the fence bordering 'Bank House', but to their surprise, they found it went right to the water's edge.

"That's not right," announced Julian. "Tow-paths have public right of way and are owned by the river board. Hang on, there's a gate a few yards back there."

They followed the fence a couple of yards towards the gate and tried to open it; to their surprise it opened.

"Come on," encouraged Julian, "shut the gate and we'll get back on the tow-path. Although, I expect there will be another gate, in that fence on the other side of this garden."

As expected, they found another gate in the far fence. However, when they started to open the gate, somebody shouted at them, "What do you think you're up to! This is private property."

Julian turned round to see who was shouting. He saw a fairly short, rotund man coming towards them.

"Are you shouting at us?" Julian asked in a quiet voice.

Caroline wondered how this was going to turn out, and decided she would let Julian deal with it.

"Don't you try and be clever with me," snapped the rotund man. "I'm a policeman and I'll have you inside for trespassing before you can blink."

"I don't think so, for one thing, you do not know who I am, and what we're doing here," Julian continued. "We are in the process of resolving several miscarriages of justice in this area; one of which is being perpetrated by you, if this is your house, which I assume it is not. However, as you are in the process of supporting this miscarriage of justice, you are guilty."

"Don't be stupid," replied the rotund man, who was starting to go rather red in the face.

"Well, for starters, this tow-path has a perpetual public right of way, which you have made very clear you want to remain fenced off. I would now like to see your warrant card to prove that you are actually a policeman, as you just stated."

"I'm afraid; I haven't got it with me."

"Now isn't that convenient; in that case, I'll need your name and number."

"My number is PC287, but I'm not giving you my name."

"That's ok. I'm sure I'll be able to get it when I meet the chief constable later in the week."

The rotund man's mouth dropped open, and he stared at Julian with his mouth open. "Come along, Caroline," said

Julian. "We have got more research to do." Then, turning to the rotund man, Julian added, "By the way, we shall be coming back this way, and I will not expect to see you here again."

They both passed through gate and continued walking along the tow-path.

Once they were out of earshot, Julian turned and smiled at Caroline and said, "That cut him down to size. I bet he is the village bully as well. By the way, did you notice his police number?"

"Yes, it's the same as the number pencilled in the monograph we got from Upper Darston."

As they continued their walk, they followed the river as it bore round to the left and found a wooden bench, which they elected to have a rest on. After short while, Julian looked at his watch.

"If we want to have lunch with Edward and Elizabeth, we should start getting back, it's eleven thirty-five," Julian announced.

"Right," replied Caroline. "I wonder if we will meet PC287 on the way back."

"It will be really interesting, if he is," retorted Julian.

Shortly 'Bank House' came into view. "Now let's see if the gate is locked."

Apprehensively, Caroline turned the gates handle, and to her surprise it opened.

"I am surprised," she announced.

A minute later, they arrived at the second gate, which also opened.

Caroline turned and smiled at Julian.

"You certainly made an impact back there, Julian."

They passed the terraced houses and climbed the steps back onto the road.

Julian glanced at his watch again, it was five minutes to one. "We'll be back just in time for lunch."

Fifteen minutes later, they were sitting in the lounge of 'Old Manor House'.

"Well, what exciting things you have been doing this morning?" Edward asked, who came into the lounge to join them after he heard them arrive.

"I would have called it interesting, rather than exciting. But I think I upset the local bully," Julian responded.

"I thought you were going for a nostalgic walk along the river bank? Elizabeth asked, who happened to come in to the lounge from the kitchen as Julian spoke."

"It started that way, but after we climbed down the steps to the river bank, we found that the bank this side of the river was a tow-path and went under bridge to this side of the river. It must also pass behind your house; did you know that?"

"I thought we just had a row of trees at the bottom of the garden. That is an investigation that is scheduled for after lunch," commented Edward.

"Come on, lunch is ready, continue your account as we eat," Elizabeth instructed.

They filed into the dining room, and after Elizabeth had dished the meal up, Edward said, "After the tow-path revelation, what happened next?"

"We went along the backs of the terraced houses in Church Lane and eventually came to 'Bank House', which is where the fun began."

"As you probably know, tow-paths have a permanent public right of way, but we found that the owners of 'Bank

House' had built a fence from the house right down to the water's edge, which meant we could not continue along the tow-path. To put it bluntly, that was illegal."

"Caroline followed the fence up from the river and discovered a gate in the fence, which to our surprise was unlocked. We went through, and continued along the tow-path inside the garden until we came to the fence, which was on the other side of the garden. Hoping there was a gate further up the fence; we walked up along the fence until we found it and opened it to leave."

"Suddenly, a rotund, short man shouted at us in a most unpleasant way. He then informed us he was a policeman and threatened to imprison us, which, as you can imagine, put my back up. So I announced that we were in the process of investigating some miscarriages of justices in the area: one he was in the process perpetrating."

"I informed him it was the act of blocking the tow-path. By this time, his face was rather on the bright red side. Hoping I had put him on his back foot, next asked to see his warrant card, which he announced he didn't have on him."

"Consequently, I asked him for his number, name and address. He responded by saying his number was 287, but he wouldn't' give us his name and address; by doing that, I'm fairly sure he thought he had outsmarted us."

"The coup-de-grace was when I said it wasn't a problem, because I'm sure the chief constable will be able to tell me what it is, when I see him next week. It left him with his face bright red and his mouth wide open."

By this time, they had migrated into the lounge.

"You were right to call him the village bully, because I have had some miner skirmishes with him, but because I knew the law better than him, they never came to court, which really got up his nose," Edward concurred. "Do you want to come and find this tow-path?"

"You go off hunting. Are you going as well, Caroline?"

"No, I'm staying in here with you, if that's ok?"

Once Edward and Julian had got to the bottom of the garden, Edward said, "I have never been this far down the garden before."

"Let's hope there aren't any lions and tigers hiding down here," Julian joked, smiling at Edward.

"Wouldn't that upset the village busybodies?" Edward smiled back.

"Edward, would you like to start up that end," Julian said pointing to the left hand end of the closely packed row of Yew trees, across the width of the back garden, and some forty feet or so tall. Julian went to the other end. A few moments later they met in the centre of the line of trees.

"I couldn't see any kind of a gap between my half of the row of trees, Julian."

"Neither could I," Julian replied. "Come on, let's look from the other side. We can get onto the tow-path from the bridge."

They walked from the house down Love Lane to Lower High Street and across over to the gate at the start of the bridge.

"Mind how you go down the steps, Edward," Julian said, holding the gate open.

They turned left when they reached the bottom of the steps and went under the bridge.

"I knew the river was here, Julian, but I didn't know this tow-path was."

"There's your row of Yew trees and I can't see any possibility of gap through them."

"Hang on a minute, Julian, look just past the last Yew tree; there is a gap we could just squeeze through," Edward said as he attempted to get through the gap sideways. "Come on, Julian, it opens out once you have got through."

They got through to the other side of the gap and walked single file along a narrow path that lead parallel to the hedge marking the boundary of Edward's house. The path suddenly turned right into a heavily wooded area, which in turn ended at a metal covered door located in a brick built single story building, about twenty foot square without windows.

"What's in there, Edward?" Julian asked. "It's obviously locked."

"I haven't seen it before, and it not on any of the land deed maps associated with the house. Let's go back to the house and see if it's on any of the other maps we have."

Having arrived back from their exploration of the tow-path at the back of the house, Edward went off to hunt in his study for a large scale map of the house and its surrounding area.

"I went through to the lounge to join Elizabeth and Caroline."

"How did you get on round the back of the house?" Elizabeth inquired.

"Well, there's no entrance from your garden on to the tow-path," Julian replied. "However, we did find a path that lead up the side of your house, which eventually led to an old single story building with no windows, and was securely locked with a modern padlock."

"The oldest map I've got for this area is an Ordnance Survey, seventh series, one-inch map, published around 1960. It shows the house, but the area where that building is located is blank," Edward announced, as he came in from his study.

They all gathered round the map and postulated a variety of solutions for the building not being on the map and what its uses were.

Suddenly, Caroline chimed in. "How about if we go to the library tomorrow? They are bound to have a large scale map of the area and perhaps some other information about that building."

"That sounds a very good idea," responded Edward. "Now who would like an alcoholic drink to round the afternoon and evening off?"

The drinks helped; the afternoon and evening become a pleasant, mellow and convivial time.

It was just after nine thirty, Monday morning, when Julian and Caroline arrived at the library.

"Is it possible to see Jane Perry, please," Julian asked the woman at the reception desk in the lending part of the library.

"Hang on a moment," the woman said as she picked up the phone and dialled a number. "Who shall I say wants to see her?"

"Julian Drake and Caroline Dobbs."

"Thank you. Hallo, Jane, I have a Julian Drake and Caroline Dobbs out here who would like to speak with you...Right, I'll send them through." She replaced the phone receiver. "If you go through to the administration office by the front door, she will see you there."

"Thank you very much," Julian replied.

They made their way back to the front, knocked on the door marked administration office, and went in.

Chapter 16

"Good morning to you both," Jane said as she met them. "Come through to my office."

They made themselves comfortable in her office. "Now what can I do for you?"

"I hope we aren't interrupting anything important."

"Nothing that cannot wait."

"We wondered if you have a two and a half inch or six-inch ordinance survey map of the area round the house where we are staying."

"Can I ask why?"

"Of course you can. On Sunday morning, we went for a nostalgic walk along the tow-path on the river bank. After we returned and had lunch, Edward and I went and explored the garden to see if there was an entrance leading through to the tow-path behind the garden, which Edward didn't know was there. Unfortunately, there wasn't an entrance."

"Subsequently, Edward and I decided to look at the garden from the tow-path side, again there was no entrance into the garden. However, there was a gap in the hedge which lead down the outside of the side hedge of the house. This path lead to a single story building with no windows, but had a door that was secured with a modern padlock."

"I see. Let me guess, you want to know about that building."

"Yes, we would like to, and wondered if you could help."

"Well, let's go and start with the maps. We need to go up to the reference library."

We followed Jane up to the reference part of the library and over to a wooden cabinet full of long thin draws, she opened the third one down and rummaged through the maps it contained.

"This one should have it on," Jane said, as she placed one of the maps on the top of the cabinet. "A six-inch ordinance survey of the area of the around where you are staying."

Julian and Caroline stood either side of Jane and peered at the map. "There's the house," Julian said pointing at the outline of the house. "The single story building should be on that side of it," and pointed to where he thought it would have been, but it wasn't marked. "It's not there. Jane, do you know why it's not there?"

"I think you are too young to remember seeing buildings and plots of land fenced off with a notice saying something like 'Private Keep Out, Ministry of Agriculture and Fisheries property'."

"We haven't seen anything like that," Julian and Caroline responded.

"I didn't expect you to. It started to be used sometime during the World War I and stopped being used between the sixties and eighties. It basically meant the 'Ministry of Defence'. In some cases, depending on their importance, they weren't put on maps, which seems to have been the case with this building."

"In that case, it raises the question—what was so important about this building," inquired Julian.

"Are there any aerial photographs that were taken of the area during the World War II, or just after, which could give us a clue?" Caroline asked.

"Hang on, yes, there was an aerial survey in the late 1940's or early 1950's, something to do with war damage I think. Now where were the pictures put?"

Jane started to rummage through a row of four-draw filling cabinets. "This is it!" Jane exclaimed as she pulled a box file out of one the draws and placed it on the table with the maps.

Julian thumbed his way through the stack of 10x8 photographs in the box.

"This is what we are looking for," he said as he placed four of the pictures on the map, which showed the house.

"If you put them in the right order, you can see where the aircraft flew along the river. Look there's the house," pointing at the second picture in the sequence. "Yes, look, there is our mystery building next to it. Also, there's somebody on the path that leads to the building and a barge is tied up against the tow-path on the river."

"Can you make out what's being taken out, or put in the building?" Caroline asked.

"No, all I can make out are boxes, but the writing on the boxes is too small to read."

"There's also a police man watching what's going on," interjected Jane. "I can see his shoulder number, but I cannot read it because it's too small."

"We need a magnifying glass," suggested Caroline.

"There's one in my office, I'll go and get it." A few moments later, Jane was back.

Focusing the glass over the policeman in the photograph, she exclaimed, "287! I know that number."

"So do we," chimed in Julian.

"He's our local policeman now, and a nasty piece of work he is to."

"We found that out yesterday morning, when I made him look very stupid."

"He wouldn't have liked that," responded Jane. "He's probably looking for way to get his own back on you."

"Thanks for the warning."

"Going back to the picture; that means PC287 knows exactly what was in the building then, and what is going on now," Caroline pointed out.

"Is there date on the back of the picture?" Julian asked. Jane turned the picture over.

"Yes, 1956," she added. "As he looks about fifty or so years old now, he must have joined the police force as early as he could, which I believe was nineteen years old then. By the way, did you know he was married to the woman who runs the post office?"

"No, we don't, though if we did I've forgotten."

"Julian, we have to go to the bank," interrupted Caroline, "to look at the bank's archive material."

"Wow, lucky you remembered, I had forgotten all about that. Jane, thank you so very much for all the help you have given us and I'm sorry we have got to rush off. By the way, do you know the name of PC287?"

"I'll look it out while you're gone and you can come back for it after you have had fun at the bank."

They strode out of the library and along to the bank.

"I'm Julian Drake and this is Caroline Dobbs, we've come to see the archivist. Sorry we are a bit late, but something came up yesterday that needed to be dealt with first thing this morning."

"That's alright, you are expected. Please come through," the receptionist said, opening the access door.

Julian and Caroline followed the receptionist through to the back of the office.

After knocking on a door marked 'Records', she introduced them to a woman, who looked in her early thirties. "This is Julian Drake and Caroline Dobbs."

"Welcome to my domain," the archivist said, as she shook their hands. "Please come and sit over here," indicating two chairs next to a desk, whilst she walked round to the other side of the desk.

"I'm not sure what I can help you with. Mr Cole asked me to show you the records from around the time Mr John Henry Hewett died, which was about 1964 I've been told, Unfortunately, I didn't work here then. However, I have retrieved records from a couple of years either side of that date."

"This pile of records are Mr Hewett's financial records for those four years, this pile consists of letters and other documentation relating to Mr Hewett. I have also managed to find several pictures taken in and around the offices at that time."

"Thank you for all the work you have done on our behalf," commended Julian.

"It was my pleasure; it has been nice to do something different. I'll leave you to search through these documents. By the way, there is copier over there, if you need to use it."

"Thank you very much."

"Julian, what shall we look at first?"

"I think a look at the pictures first would be helpful."

"There are four of them; as they are dated on the back, I've put them in date order. That one is the earliest," Caroline said, pointing at the one on the left-hand end of the row of pictures. "It's dated a couple of years before Dad's death."

"Is there one dated the same year as Dad's death?"

"Yes, the third one along."

"That is Mr Cole at one of the desks, so that must be Dad at the other. They both have piles of papers; they seem to be working through."

"Look, each of them has a cup and saucer on their desk."

"Trust a woman to notice that, although, having said that, I wonder who would have made the tea, or whether they took it in turns."

"Shall I take a copy of it?"

"Yes, that's a good idea," said Julian, as he started looking through the pile of documentation.

"How are you getting on?" Mr Cole asked, as he came into the room.

"We have just started looking at the documentation," replied Julian.

"Mr Cole, could I ask a rather trivial question?" Caroline asked.

"Of course you can."

"When we looked through the pictures, we found one showing yourself and Mr Hewett siting at your desks. On each of the desks were a cup and saucer. I just wondered who made the tea, or did you take it in turns?"

"Show me the picture."

Caroline retrieved the relevant picture from the pile and gave it to Mr Cole.

"I was intrigued by the fact that they were a cup and saucer—very posh, by today's standards any way."

"I see what you mean, it looks as if its staged, doesn't it. In answer to your question, as far as I can remember when one of us wanted a drink, we just went and made one for both of us. Does that answer your question?"

"Yes, thank you, sorry it was such a trivial question."

"I wish all the questions I get were that easy to answer. Before you think of a harder question, I'll leave you to it."

"Thank you, Mr Cole," Julian and Caroline responded in unison.

Julian continued looking through the documents but found nothing significant.

Caroline started sorting through the financial paper work, again nothing significant was found. However, there was an unusual invoice from an overseas pharmaceutical company for some unspecified chemicals.

"Julian, have a look at this," Caroline asked. "It's unusual, but is it significant?"

"Let me see, well it is dated nine months before Dad's death. I don't know if it's significant or not, perhaps I'm being over suspicious, but I think I'll copy it in case."

It took them about another hour to work their way through the rest of the financial material and the final documentation.

"Hallo, how are you getting on?" The archivist asked, who had just come into the room.

"Actually, we have just about finished," replied Julian.

"Did you find anything of interesting?"

"We copied one of the pictures, as it showed Mr Cole and Mr Hewett working side by side at their desks, out of interest. Also an unexpected invoice from an overseas pharmaceutical company, out of curiosity."

"Can I see it?"

"Of course you can, here you are. Perhaps you can give us some further information about it."

"It is certainly unexpected for a bank to be ordering from a pharmaceutical company. Unfortunately, I do not have any further information about it, not even the letter making the initial order. Sorry."

"That's all right, our curiosity got the better of us. Thank you very much for the help you have given us. Please, would you convey our thanks to Mr Cole?"

"I certainly will and hope you are successful with your future research."

"Thank you, cheerio."

"Good bye."

They let themselves out of the bank and made themselves back the library and located Jane.

Chapter 17

"Hello, both of you, how did you get on at the bank?"

"We've ended up with two more questions and no answers," replied Caroline.

"Why is that?"

"First, we found a picture of Dad and Mr Cole sitting at their desks, which seems to be a bit staged because of the two cup and saucers."

"Let me see. Yes, I see what you mean. What is the other question?"

"Look at this," said Julian, handing Jane the pharmaceutical receipt.

"Now that is strange," remarked Jane, after a pause.

"What do you make of it?" Julian asked.

"I certainly wouldn't expect a bank branch to ordering chemicals from, what I assume is, a large overseas company."

"Exactly what we thought, and it being dated just nine months before Dad's death, makes it even more mysterious!"

"That is certainly something that needs investigating. Moving on, I have an answer to one of your questions."

"What's that?"

"The name of PC287 is Mr Peter Robinson. An additional bit of news is that the lady in the post office is Mrs Robinson, they are divorced."

"Thanks for finding that out, Jane."

"Let me take a copy of that receipt and I'll see what I can find out."

"Thanks, Jane."

"It's nearly five o'clock, so I'm going to kick you out so that I can lockup. Have a nice day at the police achieve, tomorrow."

"Let's hope it will be fruitful. Bye, Jane."

The next day, after Edward, Julian and Caroline had finished their breakfast, they went outside and settled themselves in Edward's car. As Edward pulled out of the car park, Julian glanced at his watch—it was just eight o'clock.

"Julian, what are you hoping to get out of this?" Edward asked, as they turned the corner outside Jane's house and started up White Swan Hill.

"Ideally, it will have a letter saying so and so murdered Mr Hewett and dumped his body in the church, but I'm sure it won't."

"I'm almost one hundred percent certain that no such letter will exist."

"Unfortunately, I am in full agreement with you on that. However, more realistically, I do hope we will find proof that Mr Hewett was found lying dead on the church floor; not hanging on a bell rope. Perhaps some irrefutable evidence that he was murdered."

"Well, it won't be long now before we find out what is actually there."

A few moments later, Edward pulled into Grantham's police station car park. Edward took the lead as they went into the reception area.

"Good morning, I'm Mr Edward Blackmore, this is Julian Drake and Caroline Dobbs," Edward addressed the sergeant at the desk. "We have an appointment to conduct some research in your archives."

The sergeant consulted a list on the desk. "Yes, here you are, WPC Pauline Frances here has been allocated to escort you to the archive and look after you during your visit."

With that, the sergeant opened the door and let them in.

WPC Pauline Frances beckoned them to follow her through an inner door. "I'm afraid the archives are down in the dungeons."

"Is that where you keep the prisoners as well," remarked Julian.

"We did in the old days, but we are not allowed to do it now because of human rights," Pauline replied, with a grin on her face.

Having descended down a flight of concrete stairs and passed along a subterranean passage, they came to a door marked 'Archive and Evidence', which Pauline opened and bid them enter.

"This is Fred, who is in charge of this intriguing empire. Fred, this is Edward Blackmore, Julian Drake and Caroline Dobbs, who you should be expecting to spend all day messing up your wonderful filling system."

"Yes, I did read the memo," responded Fred. "Take no notice of Pauline's comments, you are most welcome here."

"I'll leave you in Fred's capable hands and come back later," said Pauline, as she left the room.

"As I understand it, you are interested in one case only: the death of a banker whose name is Mr John Henry Hewett, which occurred some twenty odd years ago."

"Yes, that is correct," confirmed Edward.

"I've put the archive box for this case and the evidence box on a table over here," said Fred, leading them towards the far end of the room. "I'll be over there in the corner, let me know if you need any help."

"We certainly will, thanks."

"Edward, you are more used to handling the stuff in the archive box, so I propose you take the lead by going through that box," suggested Julian.

"That's fine by me. Why don't you and Caroline go through the evidence box?"

"Good idea."

Silence descended on the room.

However, before Julian could get the lid off his box, Edward exclaimed, "Before you start, have a look at these case statements."

Julian started reading the first one. "It's been written by our PC287 Peter Robinson."

"Yes, in fact he has written everything that wasn't a witness statement."

"Is that usual?"

"No. It's extremely unusual."

"What does he say about when he was first associated with case?"

"Well, according to the first case report, indicated by the date, the original phone call was received at nine-seventeen in morning from the reverent Paul Jones, who said that one of his cleaners had just found a body in the church, when she had unlocked to clean the church. It says here that PC287 was contacted by phone and he arrived at the church just before ten o'clock."

"Apparently, when he arrived at the church, he found the body lying on the belfry tower floor, flat on his back. Having ascertained body was dead, he phoned the forensic team who duly arrived and took over the investigation."

"They examined the body and took numerus photographs of it, after which it was eventually taken away to the mortuary. The team then went over the surrounding area looking for relevant evidence."

"Is there an autopsy report?" Caroline asked.

"There should be one, but I haven't found it yet. I'm going to read through the rest of this stuff to see if there is anything of use for you."

Julian and Caroline opened the evidence box. It contained a wallet, some lose change, a three-piece suit, some underwear, also a bunch of keys and a pen knife.

"Wonder what the keys fit," voiced Julian to himself.

"One of these case statements indicates they fitted the bank," Edward responded to the rhetorical question.

"Are there any pictures of the body?" Caroline asked.

"Yes," replied Edward, "there's about eight from different directions. Do you want to look at them all?"

"Yes, please."

Edward gave the wad of pictures to Caroline and she started working through the pictures and passing them on to Julian.

"I don't remember Dad being that bald," Caroline said, looking at the final picture. "What do you think, Julian?"

"Let me see." Caroline passed the picture over. "Well, I certainly don't remember him having that much hair loss. Edward, is there any way we can check when he lost his hair?"

"Let me see what the autopsy report says," Edward said, as he searched through the archive box. "Here it is! That's strange, the toxicology report has been removed."

"What does that mean?" Julian asked.

"What does what mean?" A voice asked from behind them. All three of them turned round to see the owner of the voice.

"Hallo, Chief Constable, how are you?" Edward responded.

"Very well thank you, please call me Robert. Now, what does what mean?"

"Well," continued Edward, "I have just been looking at the autopsy report and discovered that the toxicology report has been removed."

"Show me," requested Robert.

Edward handed Robert the relevant paperwork.

Robert examined the documents and after several moments said, "I see what you mean. This means that without the toxicology report you cannot tell if he was or was not under the influence of drugs or had been drugged at the time he died."

"That is exactly the situation," responded Edward.

"And you two must be Julian and Caroline?" Robert inquired.

"Yes, that is correct," replied Julian.

"Please would you tell me your relationship to the deceased?"

"Yes. However, we must insist that this information will be taken as being confidential, at this point in time anyway, we are his son and daughter," confirmed Julian.

"Good. I'm assuming that you don't want your original family name made known at the moment, because there is still animosity against your family."

"Against our grandfather to be precise."

"Edward informed me that you need to have the cause of death on your father's death certificate changed to murder to resolve several miscarriages of justice. Is that correct?"

"Yes," replied Julian and Caroline in unison.

"Is Edward going to help you with the legal aspects of this quest?"

"We hope so."

"Are you going to help them, Edward?"

"Although, I have only assumed that they want me to represent them, I am planning to do so. Am I correct in this assumption, Julian and Caroline?"

"We are extremely happy for you to represent us, Edward."

"As I know Edward from the past, I will be happy to work with him on this case," responded Robert. "And I will now put this on an official standing, which means that Edward will be the interface between you, Julian and Caroline, and officialdom here at the police force."

"To start with I will allocate an experienced police officer to take charge of this case. PC287 Peter Robinson will be forbidden access in any way to this data, and any other information relating to it."

"That sounds satisfactory to me," said Edward. "However, am I correct in assuming that there will be a copy of the toxicology report located in a secure place, which PC287 Peter Robinson is ignorant of."

"Well, I wouldn't say he was ignorant of the location, he probably didn't realise that all toxicology analysis is done in a laboratory that specialises in doing that kind of analysis, which means they would have a copy of that particular analysis filed in a secure place. All I will have to do is request a copy through the correct channels and it will arrive in due course."

"Thank you, Robert, for all your help."

"I just hope that the final outcome of this case will enable you to get your father's death certificate changed to that of murder, which has proved very difficult to do in the past; mainly due to the vested interest of those who will be involved in the process being unwilling to except that they may get the blame for making a mistake. Having put that damper on things, I'll leave you find own way out."

"Thank you, Robert, for your help and cooperation. I hope it's not too long before we meet again."

Chapter 18

"How do you think that went?" Edward asked Julian, as they drove back towards the 'Manor House'.

"There was a lot less information in the boxes than I expected there to be."

"Yes, that could be for two reasons: firstly, there wasn't very much factual information to record; secondly, PC287 Peter Robinson has adjusted the information for some unknown reason. However, there was at least one good thing that I didn't find, the words murder and suicide were not found in any of the case notes or witness statements."

"I'm beginning to think that what I thought would be straight forward, is turning out to be complicated and less certain," remarked Caroline.

"Yes, it can seem like that in the early stages. However, there are several stages and refinements to go through before we get to the point where we start to make positive progress. And from what I have seen so far, Caroline, I'm sure we shall be making quite fast progress."

The tiredness due to the concentration of the day overcame them and they all settled into silence.

Suddenly Julian startled them all. "I've just remembered, Mr Samuels said we could go over to his house at one Church

Street on Wednesday afternoon, and discuss those findings he recorded in his monograph."

"That sounds like it could be interesting," said Edward.

"I hope he has identified things that haven't come to light yet."

"I wonder who his sources were," Caroline mooted.

They spent a leisurely evening after dinner, debating the various interviews and discussions they had had over the past week and a half.

"It is certainly difficult to distinguish between what is fiction and what is undisputable fact," Elizabeth commented.

"I think that several people have decided what they wanted the facts to be, even if it started off as fiction, which has resulted in the police getting the wrong end of the stick, whether they wanted to or not," Edward concluded.

"Which is going to make our research into what really happened to Dad a lot more clouded and nebulous," Julian concurred.

The next day, after a leisurely breakfast, Julian and Caroline strolled along to the library and contacted Jane.

"We're sorry to interrupt you yet again, Jane," said Julian.

"Honestly, it's not a problem, whatever the reason, even if you don't have one."

"The reason we called is, we have an interview with Mr Samuels who lives at one Church Lane, this afternoon, and then we were thinking of returning home on Thursday; but we will be coming back after a week or so. Thus we wanted to know if we should make arrangements to stay with Edward and Elizabeth through you or direct with them?"

"Make your arrangements directly with them, but I want you to promise me you will come and see me when you come back."

"We most certainly will."

"Take care of yourselves and I look forward to seeing you in a couple of weeks or so."

"Thank you for all the help you have given us and it's been a great pleasure in getting to know you, Jane."

They left the library.

"Let's go to Anne's and have lunch," suggested Caroline.

"Good idea!" The reply came.

Having finished their leisurely lunch, they dawdled their way down to Church Lane and knocked on the door of number one. After few moments, the door was opened by a woman, who Julian thought, looked younger than Mr Samuels.

"Good afternoon, I'm Julian Drake and this is my sister, Caroline Dobbs. We met Mr Samuels at his shop last week in Upper Darston and he suggested we should come round and visit him this afternoon. I hope we aren't too early?"

"No, he is here, please come in."

"Thank you."

They followed her through to what was originally the parlour.

Mr Samuels was sitting in an armchair, although he stood up as soon as they entered the room. "Thank you for coming. My name is James and my wife is Jessica."

"I'm Julian and this is Caroline, my sister."

"Please sit-down, what would you like to drink?"

"Coffee will be fine for me," said Julian.

"And for me," added Caroline.

Jessica went off to the kitchen.

"Sorry to be a bit blunt, but I don't know of any other way to put it as a book seller, why do you have an interest in the death that occurred up at the church?" Julian suddenly asked.

"Well, it's a bit of a long story. We do not originate from this area, however, we thought it was a nice area when we stumbled on it by accident."

At that moment, Jessica came in from the kitchen, with the coffee. "What have we stumbled on by accident?" Jessica asked, as she distributed the coffees.

"I was telling Julian and Caroline how we found this village."

"Yes, that was a bit of a surprise really."

"We're intrigued, aren't we, Julian."

"When Jessica and I were first married, we decided to do our combined family tree. Her maiden name is Martin and my name, as you know, is Samuels. My branch of the family tree was interesting to me, but it certainly was not exciting."

"However, when we start looking at Jessica's family tree, we discovered that she was vaguely related to the body in the church, which to us developed into an exciting event. I don't know if you have discovered that the name of the body in the church is John Henry Hewett."

"You'll be pleased to hear that we have discovered his name is the same as you have discovered, John Henry Hewett," responded Julian.

"This is exciting," commented Caroline. "How are you related to him Jessica?"

"Well, my father's name is James Martin, who married a Ruth Duckworth. Ruth had an older sister called Frances, who married a Mr Steven Henry Hewett. Steven and Frances had a son called John Henry and it was him who was found up at the church, which, if you have managed to keep track of the connections, makes me John Henry's cousin!"

Silence descended over the room and Caroline and Julian stared at each other.

It was several moments of silence before Julian spoke, "That certainly is some relationship. All the information in your monograph, James, who was the source?"

"A Mr Hewson who lives in the Bank House, just up the road towards the church, provided the balk of the information. Unfortunately, the local policeman contradicted several bits of the information, even suggesting that John Henry had killed himself."

"However, when I looked at the position of where the body was supposedly found, it looked impossible for him to have killed himself, but unfortunately, I'm not a forensic expert."

"How did you finally conclude John died, you didn't say in your monograph?"

"As I couldn't prove it either way, I decided not to make a conclusion. These days if you make a false statement in print, the lawyers see pound signs."

"What did you personally feel?"

"My gut feeling was that he was murdered, but I don't have a clue how."

"It certainly has been interesting talking with you about the murder up at the church. We have accumulated several other intriguing bits of information during our stay in the village, as well as some sources yet to get in touch with us."

"We don't know how long resolving some of these will take. When we have, would it be alright to get in touch with you again?"

"We shall look forward to it."

"Thank you and goodbye."

Chapter 19

It was just over three weeks since they had left 'The Manor House' in Lower Darston, and returned to their respective flats on the outskirts of Horsham, in West Sussex.

It was Monday morning and Caroline had come round to visit Julian in his flat. Letting herself in, she called out, "Morning, Julian."

"Morning, do you want a coffee?"

"Yes, please," said Caroline seating herself into an armchair.

"What exciting news have you brought me this morning?" Julian shouted from the kitchen, whilst making drinks for both them.

After Julian had brought the drinks in and settled himself in the other armchair, Caroline said, "Well, I have spoken to Veronica, you know my genealogist friend. She has found that George William Hewett did in fact marry; she discovered he married a Mary Ann Arundel in about 1895, and that they also had a daughter, who was born in 1897."

"Unfortunately, she hasn't managed to establish if Mary Ann's daughter married and had children. Or even children out of wedlock. However, she is still looking."

"At least, the rumour about George was true. Do you think George had anything to do with Dad's death?" Julian responded.

"I suppose it depends on how aggrieved he felt when he wasn't given any money from the family fortune, when he turned eighteen. Resentment could have festered inside his head after he left home, and eventually it could have developed into a deep desire for revenge," Caroline proposed.

"That sounds a bit unlikely. For one thing, when Dad died, George would have been around a hundred years old and even if he was still alive; he would have been unable to do anything physically," objected Julian.

"Yes, putting it like that makes it sound extremely unlikely," concurred Caroline.

Silence descended over the room as they considered the implications of the suggestions Caroline had just made, whilst they drank their coffee.

Their contemplation was suddenly interrupted by the noise of Julian's phone going off; causing both of them to jump.

"Hello, yes it's Julian speaking…how are you, Edward? Let me put this on speaker, so Caroline can hear."

"Hello, Caroline, this is Edward at the Manor House. I hope you remember me."

"Yes, I most certainly do remember you."

"I have got some good news for you both. You remember that in the case notes at the police station the toxicity report was missing?"

"Yes," they both replied in unison.

"Well, good news, Robert, the chief constable, has managed to obtain a replacement."

"Good, what does it show?"

"Your dad was poisoned with Thallium."

"I've not heard of that," said Julian.

"Neither have I," Caroline agreed.

"According to the chemist I spoke to," continued Edward, "it's a metal element, interestingly the pure metal itself is relatively harmless, which is because it is virtually insoluble in water. However, the metal salts, e.g. Thallium Oxide, Thallium Acetate and Thallium Sulphate, are toxic. The report doesn't identify which of the Thallium salts was used."

"The chemist said that the symptoms of Thallium poisoning depend on the size of the dose given to the victim. If the dose is greater than the lethal threshold, the victim will develop excruciating stomach pains and cramps accompanied by diarrhoea and other unpleasant effects, and would die within the day."

"On the other hand, a succession of small sub-lethal doses would cause flu like symptoms, which would increase in severity as the accumulation of the Thallium in the victim's body approached the lethal quantity, culminating in the eventual death of the victim, which could take weeks." Edward stopped speaking and waited for the two of them too respond.

"Well, that was quite a dissertation. Would Dad have suffered over the time it took for the Thallium to kill him?" Julian asked.

"I don't think it would have been very pleasant," Edward replied. "It also is backed up by something Elizabeth eventually extracted from Mrs Lily Jones."

"What was that?" Caroline asked.

"Apparently, Mrs Lily Jones had seen your father staggering home on evening before his death, as if he was drunk. But as she hadn't seen him drunk before, she assumed he was just unwell."

"That's about all I have got to report at the moment. Don't leave it too long before you come back up and visit us at 'The Manor House' and in view of what we have just found out, take care of yourselves. Goodbye."

"Bye, Edward, and thank you." With that, Edward hung up.

They both looked at each other.

"That was some discovery. No wonder PC287 wanted the toxicology report lost; also it would that imply, that PC287 was connected with Dad's death in some way," mooted Julian.

"It certainly implies he was involved in some way, even if it was involuntary," added Caroline.

"Let us summarise all the actual facts we now know," Julian announced after a few moments of silence.

"What are you calling an actual fact?"

"One we can prove without doubt."

"Well, we can now prove that Dad was murdered, because the autopsy report shows he was poisoned with a substance, which has such excruciating side-effects you wouldn't take it by accident. Consequently, that fact proves all the rumours concerning his suicide are false, and it also indicates the rumours about him hanging himself on the bell rope are also disproved."

"Although, it doesn't discount the possibility of the murderer stringing the corpse up on the bell rope, after he had killed Dad. We also know that PC287 had something to hide which was associated with the death of Dad, because he doctored the autopsy records."

"Can you think of anything else?"

"Only that George William Hewett had got married and had produced a daughter. But I can't see that having had an influence on Dad's death."

"I would like to return to Lower Darston and try to establish what PC287's involvement with Dad's death was. But I have no idea how we could do that, even with the help of our new friends in Lower Darston. He would need to confess, and I can't see him doing that."

"Although, it would be a golden opportunity to see how well these extra ordinary skills that Elizabeth is supposed to have can help. Julian, do you really think she is that good?"

"From the praise that Jane bestowed on her and my experience of the way she operates, I wouldn't be surprised."

Chapter 20

Caroline and Julian spent the next few weeks fulfilling various individual business obligations. Consequently, it was two months after their previous stay at 'The Manor House', when they pulled into the parking area at the front of the house. Elizabeth and Edward opened the door before they even had time to get out the car.

"Welcome back to 'The Manor House', we have really missed having you here."

"Thank you both for allowing us to stay in your house," responded Julien.

"We have both been looking forward to staying here again," added Caroline.

"Come into the lounge and make yourself at home. Edward will take your bags up to your rooms, by the way you are in the same rooms as before, I hope that's ok."

"That will be just fine," replied Caroline.

Ten minutes later, they had all gathered in the lounge and Elizabeth was in the process of distributing the drinks and concluded by placing a plate of assorted biscuits in the centre of the coffee table.

"Help yourselves!" Elizabeth chimed whilst settling herself next to Edward on one of the settees.

"Let me start by repeating what I said on the phone, it has been positively proven that your father died of Thallium poisoning," announced Edward.

Elizabeth added, "I have discovered something else from Mrs Lily Jones, which she remembered your Nan telling her shortly before your dad died, which is that your dad's hair started to fall out about three weeks before he died. Edward subsequently told me that loss of hair is also a symptom of Thallium poisoning."

"Does that mean that we now have enough evidence to get Dad's death certificate changed to murder?" Caroline asked.

"Theoretically, yes," announced Edward. "However, in practice the General Registry Office will insist on knowing why such clear evidence of poisoning was not picked up by the coroner at the original inquest, which may be difficult to explain."

"Could the coroner's report have been forged?" Julian asked.

"I'm going to arrange a meeting with the chief constable in order to find a way to establish if any of the documents could have been forged, and also try to identify what involvement, if any, PC287 had in all the falsehoods related to this case."

"Talking about PC287," Julian said, changing the subject, "did you find out anything interesting about the building next to you, particularly on your security camera?"

"All we have discovered is that PC287 visits the building about once a week, but not necessarily on the same day. Unfortunately, we have not been able to identify what, if anything, he takes away from the building."

"That's a bit disappointing. What's the possibility of breaking into the building?"

"I think I'll forget you said that, but if you decide to break into it, let me know before you do, so that the security camera will happen to have a malfunction," said Edward, winking at Julian.

"That would be unfortunate," responded Julian.

"Have you identified a day when PC287 never goes there," inquired Caroline.

"We haven't actually checked!" Elizabeth responded. "It's something we could do fairly quickly. Anyway, dinner must be about ready, so if you would like to make your way into the dining room, I'll go and dish it up."

Dinner progressed accompanied by congenial conversation which continued after they retreated to the lounge and enjoyed several glasses of a digestive until their eyes started to droop and they retired to bed.

The next morning, whilst they were all at breakfast, Caroline suggested to the others. "Shall we go and visit the library and give Jane a surprise?"

"Edward and I have nothing planned, but you won't need us anyway. You and Julian go and enjoy Jane's surprise. By the way, if it's convenient, invite Jane to dinner tonight."

"Thank you," responded Julian.

It was just before eleven o'clock when Julian and Caroline arrived at the library.

"Please could we speak to Jane Perry," Julian asked the librarian behind the counter in the lending section.

"Who shall I say is wanting to speak to her?"

"Julian Drake and Caroline Dobbs."

The librarian picked the phone up and dialled the appropriate number.

Before she had time to replace the receiver, Jane was beside them. "Julian, Caroline, it seems ages since I last saw you. Are you all right? Come into my office."

Almost instantly, they were seated around Jane's desk in her office.

However, before anyone could say a word, the door burst open and a man in police uniform came in and demanded to know what they were talking about.

"I recognise you; you are PC287 and I'm afraid you do not have a high enough security clearance to know what we are discussing," Julian immediately confronted him. "I am now going to phone my legal adviser."

He picked the phone up and dialled a number. "Hallo, this is Julian Drake, please could I speak to my legal adviser. Yes, this is Julian Drake. I am in the chief librarian's office of the Lower Darston library, having a private conversation when PC287 burst into the office and demanded to know what we were discussing."

"I then informed him that he does not have sufficient security clearance to know what we were discussing. I then phoned you…Fine, I'll wait for your arrival."

Julian replaced the receiver.

And addressing PC287 said, "My legal adviser is coming here to sort this situation out. You are to remain here until he gets here. Jane, do not say a word."

Whilst all this was going on, Julian had noticed the office door key was in the lock and had drifted over towards the door. His hand was now in reach of the key.

"I think it would be prudent to lock this door," Julian said as he turned the key.

"You can't do that!"

"I just did!"

Caroline turned her back on PC287 and smiled and winked a Jane. About ten minutes later the phone rang, Jane answered it.

"It's for you, Julian."

Julian took the phone. "Yes, knock on the door and I'll unlock it."

Julian went over to the door and waited for the knock and unlocked the door when it came.

"Come in, Edward."

Edward came in carrying a briefcase, from which he extracted an A4 notebook emblazed with OHMS Secret on the cover.

"Right, let's get started. Please lock this door. To start with I need all your names."

"I'm Julian Drake."

"I'm Caroline Dobbs." "I'm Jane Perry."

"I'm PC287."

"No, I need your full name." "I'm not going to tell you!"

"Ok, I'm not arguing, I'll find out another way." With that, he picked up the phone and consulted a small notebook full of phone numbers.

"Is that you, Robert…good this is Edward. I am currently interviewing a PC287, but he is refusing to give his full name…Good I'll hang on…Peter Robinson. Lovely, sorry for disturbing you, speak to you soon."

"Right, that's sorted."

"Now, I now need to see the warrant that has given you authority to burst into this office and demand to know what is being discussed."

PC287 stared at Edward in silence. "Come on, I need to see that warrant." Again silence.

"From your attitude, I am assuming you, in fact do not have a valid warrant to produce, which means you were in the process of conducting what boils down to be a false arrest. You can leave now but you haven't heard the last of this. Let him out."

After PC287 had left, Julian and Caroline looked at each other with big grins on their faces, but Jane had an open mouthed look of astonishment.

"Did I make a good enough legal adviser?" Edward asked.
"Perfect," Caroline pronounced.

"I'll see you back at the house," with that, Edward left.

"May I ask what happened just now?" Jane asked.

"Having brushed against PC287 last time we were here in the village. I consequently knew we needed him to think he was up against something he would come out the looser," replied Julian.

"However, to put your mind at rest, Edward is a very well-known semi-retired barrister in London and occasionally plays golf with the chief constable."

"I obviously knew Edward, from having helped him out previously, but I was unaware that his profession was that of a barrister and being on first name acquaintance with the chief constable, certainly moves him up the scale of my respect for him," responded Jane.

"If you have any trouble what so ever from PC287 in the future, either phone me or Edward at once. We think he is involved in some way with the death of our father, but we are not sure how yet. Of course, we may be wrong about this and he is in fact, just a nasty person," continued Julian.

"I almost forgot in all the excitement," Caroline suddenly interjected. "Elizabeth asked me to ask you to come to dinner with us tonight."

"Tell her I would love to come."

"We will tell you everything we have discovered tonight at dinner," Julian said. "We've taken up most of the morning dealing with PC287, so we'll leave you to enjoy the afternoon, as best you can."

"Thank you; and I'll see you at dinner later."

With that, Julian and Caroline left Jane's office and went out through the front door.

"What do you think PC287 was hoping to get out of his little charade this morning?" Julian asked, as they walked down Lower High Street.

"I have no idea, not even a guess. Let us go and have some lunch and see some friendly faces," Caroline replied.

They let themselves into the 'The Manor House' and went directly into the lounge.

Almost immediately, Elizabeth came out of the kitchen. "I hear that you were involved in a confrontation with PC287. Edward's up in his study. I'll make you a coffee; it will help settle your frustration, if that's the right word."

"It's not the word I would use," Julian mumbled. Elizabeth grinned at him, as she went into the kitchen.

Coffee and biscuits duly arrived accompanied by Elizabeth, and as if by magic, Edward arrived in the lounge at the same time.

"We can't let you two out by yourselves without you both getting into some kind of trouble," voiced Edward with a smile, as he settled himself into his chair.

"We thought it would liven your dull lives up," commented Caroline. "Being serious for a moment, Edward," expounded Julian. "What do you think PC287 was hoping to get out of that intrusion?"

At that moment, Jane arrived. Elizabeth showed her into the lounge. "You are just in time to hear what Edward thinks PC287 thought he would achieve by bursting in like he did."

"Well I can think of two possibilities. One: realising it's your second visit to the village; he was desperate to know why you were here again and hoped that because he was a policeman, you would just tell him, so that you would keep out of trouble."

"Two: by bursting in, you would be frightened into telling him. However, by making him believe it was a security problem, way above his security clearance level, he panicked. How does that sound?"

"Shame we cannot prove ether of them," Julian observed. "Lunch is ready!" Elizabeth called from the kitchen.

Chapter 21

"Can Caroline and I go through the tapes from the security camera, to see what PC287 has been up to?" Julian asked, as they sat in the lounge after lunch.

"Elizabeth has looked through some of them, but I haven't, so I would like to look through them with you?"

"Of course you can, come on."

They went up to the small box room at the back left-hand corner of the house.

"Get the spare T.V. from the spare room; it's bigger than the one with the recorder, so it will be easier for us to watch," suggested Edward.

Edward connected all the cables and put the first tape in the recorder. It took about a half-hour to go through each day on the tape.

"It's going to take us ages to get through the couple of months of tape we have," Edward mooted.

"Is there any way we can speed it up?" Julian asked.

"Give me the handbook for the recorder and I'll have a look," requested Caroline. "I would think there's a way of speeding the replay function up."

After about seven or eight minutes, Caroline said, "Found it. If we set the picture to what the instructions call 'The

Background picture', then select the 'Find Differences' button, the tape will fast forward until it finds a difference between the current picture and the one set as 'The Background picture'. Although, it warns that it may miss some small differences."

"Well done, go and see if you can make it work," Edward instructed.

Caroline removed the first tape from the recorder and placed the second one in its place and pressed the requisite buttons. Instantly, the recorder fast forwarded the tape until it suddenly stopped and displayed a picture showing a man walking along the path to the single story building.

"Who is that?" Julian asked.

"I've not seen him before!" Edward exclaimed.

"Caroline, can we print a copy of the image?" Julian asked. "Let me have another look through the handbook."

After a few moments of silence, as Caroline worked her way through the book, she exclaimed, "Yes, we can, if plug the printer in the back of the recorder and press the 'copy' button."

Edward went off and retrieved a printer and plugged it into the back of the recorder. "Try that."

Caroline pressed the 'copy' button.

The printer whirred into life and eventually produced a copy of the recorder screen.

"That's good, it's got the date, time and reference number of the original image," commented Julian.

"Let's see if we can find another," said Caroline, pressing the 'continue' button.

This time the image showed PC287, which Caroline again copied to the printer.

They spent the rest of the afternoon working their way through the pile of tapes and produced a stack of about seventy copies of various images.

"Dinner will be ready in about thirty minutes," Elizabeth's voice came drifting faintly from the kitchen.

"We had better go down stairs; bring that stack of images with you, so we can look through them after dinner," instructed Edward.

Having finished dinner and retired to the lounge, Julian started to sort the images into three separate piles, one for PC287, and two others for each of the other unknown individuals.

"Has anyone got any idea who these two unknown individuals are," asked Caroline.

"Perhaps Jane would, she has been living in the village all her life," said Elizabeth.

"I'll pop round to the library tomorrow and ask her, hopefully without PC287 intruding again."

"I'll come with you, just in case," Julian reassured her. "Now what about PC287, what days did he visit the building?"

"Well, I've looked through the pile of images and found he had been there every day, except Wednesday," commented Edward.

"I wonder what is special about Wednesday?" Julian asked. "Could one of the other two go there on Wednesdays?"

"No," said Edward. "I've checked all the other images and none are dated Wednesday."

"So Wednesday sounds like a good day to go visiting. I wonder how we could get that door open. Hang on, it's

Wednesday tomorrow, I'll go for a walk in the afternoon and see what I can see."

"I think, tomorrow afternoon I will need to readjust the surveillance recorder, after we messed about with it this afternoon," Edward said, with a big grin on his face.

After breakfast, Julian and Caroline made their way to the library and subsequently into Jane's office.

"We're sorry to interrupt you again, Jane."

"Don't worry; it will make a welcome change. I hope your PC friend won't arrive this time."

"So do we, anyway, the reason we have come is to ask you if you recognise either of these two individuals?" Julian asked, as he pushed the pictures across the desk so Jane could see them.

"Well, that one is Mr Hewson, who now lives in your old house. However, that other one, I'm afraid, I don't have a clue who that is; sorry."

"Never mind, although I think it is safe to assume that whoever he is, he's a friend of Mr Hewson and also PC287. Thanks for your help, Jane."

"I just wish I could have been more helpful."

"That's alright, I'm sure we'll see you again soon," Julian said as they left Jane's office.

On the way out, Julian said to Caroline, "Let's go back to the 'Manor House' and get some refreshment, whilst I devise a plan of campaign for this afternoon."

"I think the biggest problem will be not getting caught," Caroline said, with a tone in her voice that indicated she was not sure it was a good idea.

The two of them sat in silence; Elizabeth had provided them with coffee and gone back into the kitchen.

After ten minutes or so, Julian suddenly announced, "I think I'll get to the door all right, but how will I get the door open?"

"I'll come with you and show you," Edward suddenly announced, having come into the lounge without being noticed.

"How will you do that?" Julian inquired.

"I'll just say I was not always the bastion of the law I am now," he said with a big grin on his face. "If we go now, it will reduce the liability of getting caught, in my experience crimes are less likely to be conducted over lunch."

"You two will make grand couple of criminals," chimed in Caroline. "Come on, Edward, we better go before Caroline phones the local newspaper to get a reporter to cover the whole event."

Julian and Edward walked slowly round from the front of the 'Manor House' to the tow-path and then through the small gap in the trees to the door of the windowless building.

"Right, now show me how you are going to open this security padlock."

Edward took a small black leather pouch out of his inside pocket; opened it to reveal several probes about seven or eight inches' long, each with different shaped ends.

"Are they skeleton keys?"

"It might be better if you forget you saw them," Edward said as he progressively manipulated the probes into the padlock, until there was a click and the lock opened. "That's how it is done."

"That's a useful skill."

"It used to come in handy when I was younger."

"Let's get the door open," said Julian, removing the lock and pulling the door open.

"Did you bring a torch," asked Edward.

"No, I forgot."

"Good job, I remembered one."

Edward switched torch on and they both entered the dark interior. Even with the light from the torch, it took several moments for their eyes to get accustomed to the low level of light.

"Look there," Edward said pointing the torch to the far end of the space. "A stack of empty wine bottles, it must have been some party to have that many empties."

"They aren't used bottles, they are new, and look they don't have labels or remnants of the cork covering round the neck."

Edward swung the torch round. "What are those white plastic containers along that wall?"

"They look like they are twenty litre containers. What's inside them?"

"Hang on, there must be a light switch somewhere in here, there are no windows."

Edward swung the torch around until its beam lit up the light switch located near the door.

"There we are," Julian said, as he switched the lights on, which illuminated the whole room. "Now we can see what they are up to."

They worked their way round the room. Beside the stack of new wine bottles, there where machines for corking bottles, sticking labels, putting the foil round the cork and several other machines they couldn't work out what those were used for.

There was also a kind of desk area that had several piles of labels of expensive wines. They then realised that this was the base for a wine scam, where cheap wine was blended to taste like the expensive wine on the labels.

"I don't think we should stay here any longer because I think that the money being generated with this setup could mean the perpetrators would not hesitate to use a gun to keep it secret," Edward observed.

They switched the lights off, shut the door and reset the lock.

"I think the coast is clear," Julian whispered, looking cautiously round the end of the bushes leading onto the tow-path.

"Thanks, Julian," said Edward, as they strolled slowly along the tow-path towards the bridge. As they reached the bridge, a man came down Lower High Street in a bit of a hurry, swung on to the tow-path, just missing the pair of them.

"That was close," observed Edward.

"Yes, but did you recognise who it was?" Julian whispered in Edward's ear.

"No."

"It was the third man; whose name we don't know."

By this time, they had turned into Love Lane, and a few moments later, were in the house.

Edward poured himself a whisky. "Here you are, I think you will need one after that."

"It was certainly close."

"What was close?" Elizabeth asked.

As she and Caroline came in to the room.

"What we are about to tell you must not be mentioned to anyone outside the room," Edward commanded.

The two women looked shocked.

Edward, with help from Julian, explained what had happened to them and what they had discovered.

"What are we going to do now?" Elizabeth inquired.

Chapter 22

"The short answer is nothing; do not even mention it to Jane. Because, if she accidently lets out that she knows what is going on in that building, it would certainly be detrimental to her wellbeing."

"Let us now forget all about the goings on, in the building next door, and focus on the facts that relate, in some way, to your father's death."

"Elizabeth, would you make notes, as we agree on each fact."

"Yes I can do that; I hope it doesn't become a shouting match though." "Edward, would you be chairman?" Julian asked.

"I would love to."

"Firstly, we know that he was murdered by poisoning with Thallium." "But that is about all we can prove."

"But we do know that PC287 has been involved with Dad's death, because he was the officer involved with his case. Also, he made the toxicology report go missing."

"Good point."

Suddenly Julian went silent, which lasted for several minutes; the rest of them stared at him, wondering what he was thinking about.

"Are you all right?" Edward eventually asked. The pause continued.

"I have just had an interesting thought, although improbable," said Julian, suddenly coming to life.

"Come on then, enlighten us."

"That aerial picture that Jane has in the library was dated around 1956. Consequently, PC287 was in all probability involved in the wine scam shortly after that date, if not already. Dad died in 1964, a few years after the scam. Consider if Mr Hewson, who was one of the perpetrators of the wine scam, coveted 'Bank House' for himself."

"After Dad died, is it possible Mr Hewson blackmailed PC287 with his involvement in the wine scam, to make Dad's death look like suicide in order to get 'Bank House' at a knockdown price."

"What on earth are you talking about?" Caroline exclaimed. "Where did that idea come from?" Edward asked in amassment.

"I don't know, it just popped into my head. But it does seem a plausible idea. However, the seemingly insurmountable problem is: how could we prove it, if it is true."

"The only way I can see is if PC287 was to confess to being blackmailed and subsequently adjusting the evidence of your dad's death to make it look like suicide," suggested Edward.

Silence descended throughout the room.

"Anyone for coffee?" Elizabeth's voice suddenly broke the silence. "Yes," everyone replied in unison.

Coffee arrived and everyone sipped their drink and pondered, what they hoped would be a fool proof way of trapping PC287.

"Well," Caroline continued, "PC287 knows he adjusted Dad's death documentation so that it looked like suicide, but he doesn't know we know."

"Edward, what would happen to him if it became public knowledge?" Caroline asked tentatively.

"I think he would be thrown out of the police force and as I suspect his house is a police house, he would lose his house. That would be without considering whatever criminal charges would be imposed."

"In that case then, could we blackmail him into providing information about Dad's death, by threatening to make his involvement in modifying the evidence of how Dad died known publicly."

"If we were to involve Robert and the police force, it will mean the Police Federation also becoming involved and they would stop PC287 saying anything that might incriminate himself. And that is just what we want him to do."

"I have an idea!" Elizabeth interjected. "PC287 knows you three are up to something, but he doesn't know me. What about if I casually make friends with him and somehow get him to agree to an informal meeting somewhere. Mind you, I don't know how yet."

"Do you think you could?" Julian asked.

"The worst that would happen is that he gets nasty, meaning we fail to get any information and we are back at square one."

"He may get you locked up," Caroline pointed out.

"But with Edward on my side, I don't think it would be for very long." "Elizabeth, you have a lot of faith in my abilities."

"I've seen you at work in a court remember."

"O' that reminds me, I've got to go and attend court in London next week. So I will be away for the best part of a fortnight."

"Good; that will be a good opportunity for us to go home for a week or two, in order to attend to various business situations," Julian informed them. "How long will your court case take?"

"Between five and seven days."

"Good. That means you will be back about the same time as us. Elizabeth, would it be alright if Caroline and I leave in the morning?"

"Of course it will. Perhaps I will have made some progress with PC287 by the time you get back."

The next morning, after Julian and Caroline had left, Elizabeth sat down with Edward.

"I know I sounded very glib yesterday when I said I would chat up PC287, but this morning I'm not so confident. Could you give me some guidance on how to proceed, Edward."

"Try to approach him when he's relaxed, perhaps when he's having a coffee or a beer. Keep it short, especially for the first occasion. I'm sure that you have much more experience in progressing the conversation from then on."

Eventually, Monday morning arrived. Edward had left early for London, leaving Elizabeth alone in the house.

"I'll walk up to the library and tell Jane, Julian and Caroline have gone back home, but will be back in a fortnight," she said to herself.

She was just entering the library when PC287 shot past her in the direction of White Swan Hill. Elizabeth rushed up to the first floor of the library and found the window that looked out towards White Swan Hill.

She was just in time to see PC287's car pulling into the White Swan pub car park.

"That was fortunate," Elizabeth said out loud to herself.

"What was fortunate said a voice behind her." Elizabeth, spun round to find Jane standing there.

"O' it's you. Hallo, Jane, I've just seen PC287 pull into the White Swan pub. I had been wondering where he had his mid-morning coffee or lunch, and now I know. I just popped in to tell you that Julian and Caroline have had to go home for a couple of weeks, but will be back in a fortnight."

"As I'm going to be alone for the next week and half, I thought I would do some snooping of my own. As PC287 doesn't know me, I thought I might accidently bump into him and I have heard that the White Swan pub is fairly nice to drop into." Elizabeth gave Jane a wink.

"I have never been in there, so I can't comment," Jane replied with a smile. "Good luck."

Elizabeth left the library and started walking up towards the White Swan.

As she walked across the car-park, she noted there were only four cars parked and assumed that one of them would be the landlords, which indicated there would not be many customers in the pub; this was confirmed as she entered the bar.

"Can I help you?" The barman asked. "Yes, please, I'd like a vodka and orange." "Certainly."

Elizabeth glanced round the room; there was a total of five individuals, two were obviously together. As her eyes scanned round the room, she noted without staring, where PC287 was sitting alone at a corner table.

"Here's your drink, madam. It's quite an old fashioned drink." "Thank you, I haven't found another drink I'd prefer."

"I haven't seen you here before."

"No, my husband is tied up for a couple of weeks, so I've decided to do a little exploring around the area."

"I hope you have a nice time."

Elizabeth moved over to a table on the opposite side of the room to PC287 and sat in a chair that enabled her to watch him, without it being obvious she was watching him.

As time passed, she noticed he kept glancing at her. After half an hour, she ordered another drink and a food menu.

She went over to the bar. "Can I order some fish and chips please?" "Of course you can, it'll be about twenty minutes, and I'll bring it over when it's ready."

"Lovely."

However, she noticed PC287 slowly sauntering over to the bar and stood next to her.

"Hallo, are you here on holiday?"

"No, just exploring, whilst I have the opportunity."

"Well, I'm the local police officer, if there's anything I can help you with, do not hesitate to ask."

"Thank you," with that Elizabeth went back to her table and her meal duly arrived.

However, throughout all this Elizabeth kept her eyes on PC287 and noticed he was paying more attention to her, almost watching her continually.

I think I'll call it a day. I seem to have caught his interest, Elizabeth thought to herself as she got up and went to the bar to pay.

"Thanks for coming. Will we see you again?"

"I can't see why not, goodbye," Elizabeth said as she started towards the exit.

"Can I give you a lift?" PC287's voice came across the room.

"No, thank you," replied Elizabeth, without turning towards him; and strode out of the pub, across the car-park towards the library.

I don't want him to follow me home, so I'll hide in the library, Elizabeth thought to herself.

A few moments later, she entered the library, went up to the first floor and looked through the various windows to see if PC287 was following her.

"How did your accidental foray go?" Jane asked, with a smile.

"It went very well, except that right at the end as I was leaving, he wanted to give me a lift home, which I certainly didn't want him to do, as I don't want him to know where I live. I was looking to see if he was following me. Hang on, there he is, parked over by the hotel."

"He must have seen you come in here, well you certainly can't go out the front door, but I have a cunning plan."

"You have a witches' spell book with which you can make me invisible," Elizabeth said laughing.

"Not quite, but as good as. Come with me."

Jane lead Elizabeth towards the back of the first floor, where there was a door that looked like it hadn't been opened for a considerable time.

Jane took her bunch of keys and searched through them until she found a rusty looking one, which she used to unlocked the door. "This is my secret passage, be careful it's dark." She ushered Elizabeth through the door and relocked it behind them. There was a small window that let just enough light in, so they could see where they were going.

"Mind these stairs, they're a bit steep."

Eventually, they arrived in a small room with two doors, one lead back into the library and the other was obviously an outside door, which Jane unlocked.

"This was part of the servant's access to the rest of the house, when it was originally used as a house, but it's not used now and has been forgotten about by everyone else," Jane said as she relocked the door.

"We are now in the old back garden and somewhere down here is an old path that leads to Love Lane."

Jane lead the way along a much over grown path which was once the rear access to the house, ultimately they came out onto Love Lane, about a hundred yards from 'The Manor House'.

"Now that is a surprise," Elizabeth commented.

"The road's clear, if you go now, I'll go back this way and leave by the front door, which should throw PC287 into a bit of confusion."

"Thanks so much, Jane."

Chapter 23

The next day, Elizabeth, still feeling a bit shaken by how strong PC287 came on to her yesterday, was sitting in the lounge contemplating what to do next; she was halfway through her second cup of coffee, when a plan started to form in her mind.

I think I need someone to talk this through, Elizabeth thought to herself. "Tomorrow is Wednesday, which is half-day closing for the library."

Picking up the phone, she dialled the library's number. "Could I speak to Jane Perry please…Thank you, I'll wait…Jane, is that you? It's Elizabeth…I was wondering if you were busy tomorrow afternoon after the library had closed. I have something I want to pass by you, to see what you think."

"I'll prepare some dinner for us both, you could also stay the night, if you wish, there will only be me here…You will come, good…Try not to let PC287 see you arrive…Thanks, goodbye."

It was about two o'clock on Wednesday when a knock on the door sent Elizabeth rushing to the front door hoping to see Jane.

"You look a bit flushed," commented Jane as she entered the hallway.

"Am I. Probably the rush to open the door, I didn't sleep that well last night either. Come and sit down, I'll get us a drink."

"Are you all right?" Jane asked as she followed Elizabeth into the kitchen.

"No, not really, yesterday certainly got to me in a way I wasn't expecting."

"Let me carry those cups, you're a bit shaky."

"Thanks."

"Now when you're ready, tell me the details of what happened to get you in this state."

They sat in silence whilst they drank their coffee.

Eventually, Elizabeth started. "It was the last part, as I was leaving the pub. He started to come on a bit heavy and asked if he could give me a lift home. Then, when I got home it hit me, the enormity of what might have happened, if I hadn't hidden in the library."

"I felt in need of someone to talk too, which is when I phoned you. And am I pleased you've come."

"You sounded very flustered when you called, which wasn't like you, so I thought I'd better come."

"When did he leave the hotel?"

"He was still there when I went home about five o'clock, which gives us an idea of how persistence he is. Now I understand what is making you so worried."

"Thanks for your concern."

"Right, let us now work out a plan of attack. What is it you're trying to achieve?"

"The original plan was for me to get chatty with PC287 and convince him it would be a good idea for him to confess that he changed the evidence of John Hewett's death, so it looked like he committed suicide rather than murder. I didn't expect him to come on to me so hard, that it caused me to panic."

"You certainly under estimated your victim."

"Don't remind me, can you think of a way we could get back on track?" "Do you think he sees you as a lonely housewife, looking for a short affair whilst your husband as away?"

"If he does, then he won't have suspected what my real motive is."

"Right, as I'm staying to night, I will go to the library at the normal time via the back way. At about eleven thirty, I want you to come in via the back door, go up the stairs to the first floor, just in case PC287 decides to wait in the lobby by the front door, I'll leave both doors unlocked. Then we'll walk up to the White Swan pub and have a drink or two and some lunch."

"Hopefully, PC287 will be there, or come in whilst we are there, and you can ask what he knows about the 'Hanging Banker'. If it goes to plan, and with a bit of luck, we shall find something out. How does that sound?"

"At least, there will be two of us."

As they were eating breakfast the next morning, Jane asked, "How are you feeling today?"

"A lot better, thanks. In fact, I'm looking forward to it."

"Good, I'm going off to work now, see you about eleven thirty." "You certainly will. Take care and I'll see you later."

Gauging it would take her about fifteen minutes to get to the library, she decided to leave at eleven fifteen. She arrived at the first floor of the library at almost exactly eleven thirty.

I hope Jane's there, Elizabeth thought to herself, as she opened the door. She gave a sigh of relief on seeing Jane looking out one of the front windows.

"Let me lock that door," said Jane, as she turned and walked over towards Elizabeth.

"Have you seen him yet?" Elizabeth asked.

"No, I haven't. Although, I'm not too surprised." "Shall we go now?"

"Come on then."

They both went down the stairs and out the front door and started up the hill towards the White Swan.

"What would you like to drink?" Elizabeth asked Jane when they reach the bar.

"Gin and tonic please."

"How can I help you?" The barman asked.

"A gin and tonic and a vodka and orange please."

Having got their drinks, they moved over and sat at the table Elizabeth sat at last time.

"PC287 doesn't appear to be here yet," commented Elizabeth.

Just as Elizabeth finished talking, the front door opened and PC287 walked in; he brought his drink and went and sat in the far corner, opposite Jane and Elizabeth.

"Do you think he has noticed us?" Jane asked.

"O' yes, he has noticed us all right. Give it a few moments."

"Jane, I had forgotten how intriguing trying to resolve a problem can be." "May be I can help," PC287's voice made them both jump.

"Can you?"

"It depends on what it is."

"Well," said Elizabeth, "I have been thinking about the hanging banker. You know the one who died in the church."

"In fact, I know quite a lot about the case, I was the presiding officer on the death."

"Really, then perhaps you could tell me why he is recorded as committing suicide, when in fact he was murdered."

"Who told you that!" PC287 exclaimed.

"Well, it's obvious, when you look at the place he was killed. No way could he have hung himself from where the bell ropes are located."

"Look here, I was there at the time."

"I don't think so, because I have seen documentation that says he was discovered by a cleaner and the body was lying on the floor. By the way, the document is in the public domain. So I would like to know why you lied about it."

"You are a middle-aged interfering woman and don't know what you're talking about."

"If that's your attitude, you won't mind if they reopen the case."

"Who told you that?"

"Apparently, some of his family have discovered some new evidence, which shows he could never have committed suicide. So they are bound to reopen the case."

"They can't do that."

"O' yes they can, if it's new evidence that the coroner didn't see at the original hearing. I've read enough 'who done its', to know how it works. Perhaps you did it because you were being blackmailed by someone for something you've done or are doing," Elizabeth said and then smiled at him.

PC287's face turned very pale and suddenly sat down in the spare chair next to Elizabeth and Jane.

Silence descended.

"We are going back to the library now, if you want to come and talk about it in private, come there. Perhaps we could work something out?"

With that, Elizabeth and Jane left, leaving PC287 to his thoughts.

Chapter 24

Elizabeth and Jane arrived at the library. "Come on, as we didn't get any lunch at the White Swan, I'll treat you at Anne's."

They found themselves a seat by the window and ordered their lunches. "Do you think he will come?" Jane asked.

"O' yes, he will come, but it may take a day or two, or even a bit longer, but he will come, I'm sure of it. Please phone me as soon as he does."

Their lunch arrived.

After they had finished their lunch, they walked back to the library.

"If you haven't heard from PC287 by Monday morning, give me a call and we can visit the White Swan again. And maybe we will get some lunch."

With that, Jane let Elizabeth out the back door.

It was Monday morning before Jane phoned Elizabeth. "PC287 hasn't contacted me so I'll unlock the back door for you and will see you about eleven thirty. Is that all right?"

"That will be perfect, see you then."

Elizabeth entered the library, dead on eleven thirty. "Hallo, Jane, everything all right?"

"Nothing has happened and I'm looking forward to lunch." "So am I, come on."

They left the library and walked up to the White swan.

Having ordered their drinks, they sat in the same window seat as last week.

"I notice PC287 is not here yet," commented Elizabeth.

"Do you still think he will come? I mean to the library; I'm expecting him to come for his liquid lunch."

"I must admit, I have been wrong before, but not that often. But time will tell. Do you want another drink?"

"Yes, please."

"What do you want to eat? I can recommend the fish and chips." "That will do nicely."

Elizabeth went over to the bar and ordered the drinks and two meals. She brought the drinks back to the table and after about fifteen minutes, their meals arrived.

"This is really nice fish and chips, thanks for recommending it."

"My pleasure."

At that moment, the front door opened and PC287 came in. He chose to ignore them, collected his drink and sat over the other side of the bar.

Elizabeth watched him out of the corner of her eye, whilst they finished their meal.

"It was really satisfying," said Jane. "I'm pleased you enjoyed it."

The barman came over and collected the plates. "How was it?" "It was exceptional, thank you."

As the barman left, Elizabeth noticed PC287 get from his table and walk towards them.

"Hallo," said Elizabeth. "Can we help you?"

"Is that offer you made last week still open?" PC287 asked.

"Of course it is, what day and time do you want to come to the library?"

"About ten o'clock on Thursday and I want it held in strict privacy."

"I'll get the interview room ready and we both will be waiting for you. I'll meet you at the library front door," Jane said in her most organisational voice.

With that, PC287 went back to his table.

"Finish your drink, and let's get back to the library," instructed Elizabeth. Jane made them both a cup of tea and they settled in Jane's office.

"Well, that went easier than I expected. I hope Thursday goes as easy. Although, Edward is due back on Wednesday, and I think I need to persuade him to be our on-call legal adviser; just in case PC287 tries anything funny."

"I think that is a good idea," agreed Jane.

"I'll come about nine thirty on Thursday morning, if you would let me in the backdoor at that time."

"Of course I will."

"It's about time I disappeared home, if you would be good enough to let me out."

Jane picked her keys up and the pair of them made their way to the backdoor.

"Until Thursday morning, bye." "Until Thursday, mind how you go."

Elizabeth made her way to Love Lane.

Edward arrived home on Wednesday, and was in a very good mood as he had won his case and the jury had returned the guilty verdict, after only a couple of hours. Elizabeth outlined to Edward what she and Jane intended to suggest to PC287 on Thursday morning; and he agreed to act as their on-call legal adviser.

Thursday morning found Elizabeth installed in the interview room and Jane was in the front door lobby waiting for PC287.

"Hello, PC287, or would you rather be called Peter."

"Peter will be ok," replied PC287.

"Come through, we are in the interview room. My name is Jane and this is Elizabeth. Would you like a drink, Peter?"

"No, thank you."

"Basically," said Elizabeth, "we want to know why John Henry Hewitt's death was recorded as suicide, when we have discovered he was irrefutably murdered. We have been told that you were the officiating officer, which is why we are asking you these questions."

"For instants, how did you manage to get the coroner's report and the toxicology report removed, when he would have signed the report as showing he was murdered? Tell us, how did you manage to do that?"

"In fact, that was the easiest thing to do. After the inquest, I took the coroner's report and toxicology report whilst they were in transit to the registrar and made a copy of them, then a forger I know modified the details to show Mr Hewitt as having committing suicide."

"I then put the original coroner's report and toxicology report in an envelope, put the name and number of a different case on it and slipped in the appropriate case box. The modified copies were then allowed to continue on their way to the registrar, who provided the death certificate in the usual way, showing death by suicide."

"Can you remember the name of the case where you hid the original documents?"

"No, but I have it written down at home, which I'll bring to the library tomorrow."

"Good, we will need it if we are to get you off the hook for this case. The next question is why did you do it?"

"A Mr Hewson who lives in the 'Bank House', along Church Lane, insisted that I made Mr Hewitt's death look like a suicide."

"Now what hold did he have over you which would make you put your career at risk, plus a possible jail sentence?"

"As you guessed, the other day at the White Swan, he has a hold over me."

"Could it be something to do with a windowless building along the tow-path, which runs parallel to Love Lane?" Jane asked.

"What do know about that?"

"I have discovered an aerial photograph from the mid-1950's, which shows you, and some others, carrying boxes into the building. Does that mean you and presumably the others were up to no-good?"

"The short answer is yes, but it's more than my life's worth to tell you what is going on in there."

"We will leave it at that, for now," said Elizabeth. "But there is one question I must ask you. Did you kill John Henry Hewett?"

"No, on my life, I swear I didn't kill him. He was lying on the floor when I got to him."

"I hope that is the truth," Elizabeth growled at him. "Assuming it is true, we have to make some arrangements. We will then want you to do things exactly as we tell you to do them, which means we need a private phone number we can contact you twenty-four hours a day."

"Let me write it down for you." Elizabeth gave him a piece of paper and Peter wrote the number down.

"It will probably be sometime next week before I contact you. Thanks for coming."

Jane showed PC287 out of the library and returned to the interview room.

"Jane, that went easier than I expected," commented Elizabeth.

"I'll agree with you there."

"Please would you let me out the backdoor. I need to explain all that to Edward. I don't know about you, but I still don't fully trust PC287."

"I know what you mean. Come on, I'll let you out."

Chapter 25

"How did you get on?" Edward asked, as Elizabeth joined him in the lounge.

"A lot better than I expected, in fact so much better that I'm waiting to find out what the catch is. I just don't trust PC287."

"Sit down, I'll make you a coffee, or would you like something stronger?" "I think a whisky would be the best option after this morning."

"There you are, madam, one double whisky. Right, now tell me what you have discovered and, more importantly, what have you promised to do."

"We were right; the man now living in 'Bank House' blackmailed PC287 into changing the murder evidence to look like it was suicide, so that the 'Bank House' would come on the market, as described in that legacy document, and he could purchase it really cheap."

"That makes sense."

"Fortunately, PC287 didn't destroy the original coroner's report and toxicology report; having first copied them, he just put them in an envelope, wrote a different name and case number on it and placed in the appropriate case note's box."

"Once PC287 had disposed of the originals, he took the copies to a forger who made them look like they came from a suicide case, which was then forwarded to the registrar, who produced a death certificate for a suicided case."

"PC287 must have destroyed the forgery of the toxicology report, after the death certificate had been written because it wasn't in with the case notes. Which is very clever because it removes any connection with the forged death certificate."

"However, he could produce the originals if necessary, which would then move the blame for the false death certificate onto the registrar. Do you know which case notes the original coroner's report and toxicology report have been hidden in?"

"Not yet, PC287 is dropping it into the library in the morning."

"Good, let me know what it is as soon as you can and I'll go and get the paper work from Grantham. No, second thought, I'll leave at about eight o'clock in the morning to get there early. I want you to phone the case number through to Robert, the chief constable, as soon as you can."

"I certainly will."

At just after eight o'clock, on Friday morning, Edward set off for Grantham police station. He arrived at the police station without mishap and went into the reception area.

"Can I help you?" The desk sergeant PC287.

"Yes please, my name is Mr Blackmore. I'm here to see the chief constable. He is expecting me."

The desk sergeant picked the phone up and dialled the appropriate number. "I have a Mr Blackmore at the reception desk, he says he has an appointment…I'll tell him, sir."

"Please take a seat and he will be along shortly."

"Thank you, Sargent."

"It's nice to see you, Edward," came the chief constable's voice from the side door. "Come through."

"Morning, Robert," Edward said, as he followed the chief constable along the passage and into his office.

"Take a seat, Edward, would you like a coffee?"

"Yes, please, one sugar."

Robert picked up the phone, and put in the request.

"Now, Edward, what is this urgent information you have come to enlighten me with."

"My wife, Elizabeth, has a remarkable gift. She somehow makes individual's part with information during a passive conversation, when they have no intention of doing so. What I'm going to tell you is the result of several such conversations with PC287."

"Sounds like a very useful gift to have."

"We have found it useful on several occasions. The first point is that PC287 confessed to being blackmailed into manipulating the evidence of Mr John Henry Hewitt's death, to make it look like it was suicide. Secondly, he also told Elizabeth who had blackmailed him: it was a Mr Hewson, who now lives in Bank House, located in Church Lane, Lower Darston."

"And finally, PC287 said he had hidden the original coroner's report and the toxicology report in a case box of another suicide death, so that it would be unlikely to be found, but could be produced if there was a need. He said he would let Jane have the case number and name, sometime today. Jane would then let Elizabeth know, so that she could forward it to us."

"However, Elizabeth didn't trust him. Consequently, I have come to see if I can find the case number and name, based on what we know, with your permission of course."

"I see, so you want look in the case boxes of suicidal deaths, which occurred a year or so either side of Mr Hewitt's death."

"That about sums it up," said Edward.

Robert picked the phone up and dialled a number. "Hallo, Fred, Robert here, are you very busy at the moment?…Good, a Mr Blackmore will be joining you in a few moments and would like to look at the case notes of some old suicide deaths. Is that all right?…Good, thank you."

"Come on, Edward, I'll show you the way to the archives."

"Hallo, Mr Blackmore," Fred said as they entered.

"I'll leave you in Fred's capable hands, Edward," Robert said, as he started to leave.

"That will be fine, Robert, see you later. Hallo, Fred, how are you. Sorry to invade your kingdom again."

"I'm all right, it's a pleasure to have someone to talk too. What can I do for you?"

"You remember the case of Mr John Henry Hewitt I looked at a couple of weeks ago. Well, I want to look at some suicide cases that occurred a couple of years' either side of Mr Hewitt's death."

"The suicide deaths are over here; each one should have a date next to the case number. Now, what was the date of Mr Hewitt's death?"

"1964."

"Right, here's one dated 1962."

"Let me see inside the boxes. I'm looking for an envelope with the case number on it," said Edward, as he took the boxes down from shelf.

He sorted through the papers in the box, but there was no sign of the envelope.

"It's not this one," stated Edward.

"This one is dated 1965."

Edward went through the second box without finding the envelope. "Not this one either."

"This one is 1963. It's a bit bigger than the other two."

"It certainly is; hang on what's this," Edward said eagerly pulling a foolscap envelope out of the box.

"This is it." Having pulled the documents out and spread them out on the desk. Edward read the name on the original coroner's report and the toxicity report, "John Henry Hewitt."

"But the case number on the envelope is the same as this case," commented Fred.

"Yes, but I had received information which indicated that some relative details for the Hewett case had been hidden in a different case. I guessed it would be in a suicide case."

"Good job you guessed right, otherwise we would have been here forever." "Thanks for your help, Fred."

"No problem, it made a nice diversion." "Now to get these documents to Robert."

"Hallo, Edward, did you have any joy," said Robert, as Edward entered his office.

"Voilà," Edward said, plonking the documents on Robert's desk.

Just at that moment, Robert's phone rang. "Hallo…right, just a moment. Edward, it's for you."

"Mr Blackmore speaking…Elizabeth did Peter deliver the case number…not yet, hmm…do you think he will?…I suppose he could. I'll see you later, I shouldn't be late. Bye, love."

"Good news?"

"Not really, Peter, PC287, hasn't come across with the case number where he hid the envelope containing the original coroner's report and the toxicity report of the Hewitt case as he had promised. However, having found them, makes his input superfluous."

"I'll get these documents filed in the correct box, but I will get them copied first."

"That's a good idea. You now know that Mr Hewson blackmailed PC287, well I know what he is involved in: it's a wine-scam. They buy cheap wine, then rebottle it in appropriately shaped bottles and label them as an expensive wine, which they sell at a vast profit."

"How did you find that out?"

"I'm afraid I can't tell you."

"I can imagine several reasons why you don't want to. So I won't ask."

"Is there anything else you want to know at this point?"

"No, I think you have caused enough mayhem for one day."

"That's what I like to hear, so I shall go home. Thanks, Robert, for all your help."

Edward arrived back at the 'The Manor House', and had joined Elizabeth in the lounge, poured himself a whisky, whilst Elizabeth enjoyed her coffee.

"Tell me how you got on with Robert at Grantham Police Station," Elizabeth asked, once she felt Edward had relaxed after his day out.

"Well, I decided to try and find the missing coroner's report and toxicology report by searching suicide deaths a few years either side of John Hewitt's death, and on the third box I found it, with Fred's help I must admit."

"So we don't need the name of the case box in which it was hidden from PC287."

"We don't need it, but I want PC287 to think we do. Thus, on Monday, I want you to chase him up as to why he didn't get it to you when he promised."

"Yes, I think I can lay it on a bit thick."

"Are we expecting Julian and Caroline to arrive tomorrow?"

"Yes, that reminds me, I better go and check their rooms are ready for them."

"It'll take most of the weekend to bring them up to date. I hope they will be pleased with the progress we have made. We also have to plan what we are going to do next, especially with PC287."

Saturday morning arrived at a leisurely pace. It was ten o'clock before the breakfast things had been washed up. Edward and Elizabeth sat in the lounge contemplating the rest of the day, suddenly the phone made both of them jump out of their skin.

"Hallo, yes I'll just get her…it's for you."

"Elizabeth speaking…really, what excuse did he give for being late, did he give…He forgot, as good as any I suppose. I'll come round the back and pick it up…thanks, Jane."

"Who was that?"

"Jane at the library. Guess who has just brought the name and number of the case where the envelope containing the coroner's report and toxicology report into the library?"

"Who."

"Our friend, PC287. I'm going round to the library to get it now via the back door to pick it."

"I didn't know the library had a back door."

"If you come with me, I'll show you. It has proved extremely useful whilst you've been away."

After checking the road was clear, Elizabeth led the way up to the back entrance to the library, through the back door and up the old servant stairs to the first floor, where they met Jane.

"You've brought Edward as well."

"He didn't know the library had a back door, so I thought I would show him in case he has a need to use it"

"Good thinking. I will need to know when you are coming that way, as I am the only person who has the keys and knows where the door is, apart from you two that is. Here is the envelope, take good care of it."

"We will, thank you very much. I'll let you know what is going to happen next when we know. By the way, Julian and Caroline are coming back today, so we had better get back. Thanks again."

With that, Jane let them out.

"I didn't know that access was there," said Edward, once they had returned to the lounge.

"Come on, show me these important documents," commanded Elizabeth. "Ok, just let me get the infamous envelop," Edward said, leaning across the table to reach it.

As if on cue, the door bell sounded.

"That will be Julian and Caroline," Edward said, as he got out of his chair and went to open the door.

"Look who's come to stay," Edward announced, leading Julian and Caroline into the lounge.

"Caroline, Julian, how nice to see you, sit down. You must need a drink after your journey. I'll make you a drink," said Elizabeth, heading for the kitchen.

Chapter 26

Julian and Caroline settled themselves on the sofa and Elizabeth brought the coffee in.

"We've been away a whole fortnight, which means you have discovered nothing or have solved the complete problem," Julian said with a big smile on his face.

"Neither." Edward smiled back at them.

"Come on, this sounds exciting, tell us what you have achieved."

"We have gained a confession. Though I should say, Elizabeth got the confession."

"Who from?" "Peter Robinson." "Who's that?"

"PC287."

"Let me get this clear," Julian said. "You are telling us PC287 has confessed, I'm assuming to the death of our father."

"Unfortunately, not to his death but into hiding the real coroner's report and toxicology report and replacing it with a faked set of reports, which lead to a suicide death certificate being produced through the normal channels," Elizabeth recounted.

"My first question is why?"

"That was my first question. Apparently, he was blackmailed by Mr Hewson, of 'Bank House', because of Peter's involvement with the building without windows."

"I see. How did you get him to confess?"

"Well, I told him that some of the relatives of your father had irrefutable evidence that your father was murdered and were going to request a retrial, or at least a second inquest so that the coroner will re-examine the original coroner's report and corresponding toxicology report to try and get the current death certificate changed or reissued to show that your father was murdered."

"After that, PC287 became very cooperative, even nice, and wanted to get his name taken of the case, which is the stage we are now at."

"Does that mean, we now have enough evidence to get the death certificate changed?" Julian PC287.

"I think we have, but I will need to check with the chief constable," concurred Edward.

"Will PC287 be prosecuted for falsifying evidence?" Julian asked.

"Part of getting the confession, Elizabeth promised to try and get Peter's name removed from the charge of falsifying evidence. The way I think we could do that is by getting Peter to incriminate the other two who are involved in the wine-scam in return for being exonerated from all charges."

"Because, it's been running for so long, busting the wine-scam would be a big feather in the chief constable's hat. It could also lead to catching those involved with the distribution organisation," Edward outlined.

"I think I'll phone Peter Robinson and see if he is willing to cooperate with our proposal," announced Elizabeth. "I'll use the phone in the study."

"Do you think Peter will cooperate Edward?" Caroline asked.

"From what Elizabeth has said, I think he will, but even if he doesn't, it won't stop us trying to get the death certificate changed."

Eventually, Elizabeth came back in the room. "How did you get on?" Julian PC287.

"Surprisingly, he was quite enthusiastic and looked forward to shopping the other two wine-scam operatives."

"Good. That means we can start the process of changing the death certificate on Monday, if it's alright by Edward," Julian enthused.

"We can start the ball rolling on Monday, by contacting the General Registrar Office and finding out what we have to do to start the process. But I must point out that it will not an overnight process and I suspect it will be far from straight forward."

"Forget all about that until Monday," Elizabeth's voice broke into the discussion. "Because dinner is ready and you all need to come through to the dining room."

The four of them filed through to the dining room, and the conversation for the rest of the evening consisted of more general subjects. Sunday passed without incident.

Monday morning saw Edward leaving for Grantham to update the chief constable of their plan of action.

"Hallo, Edward, I didn't expect you this morning."

"Good morning, Chief Constable. I'm sorry, I should have warned you I was coming. The reason I have popped in to see you, is because I have made a list of reasons why the death certificate of John Henry Hewett needs to be changed."

"Please would you forward it to the General Registrar Office, I thought it would look more official coming via you. I have also put a covering letter in the envelop, which I have left unsealed so that you can examine my reasoning."

"I'm sure it will be perfect, but I will check it before forwarding it. However, knowing your past, I doubt if there is even a full-stop out of place."

"Thank you, Robert. By the way, PC287 has agreed to cooperate over the wine-scam."

"That will be very helpful, there have been several rumours over the years that some kind of wine-scam is going on, but unfortunately never any concrete evidence."

"I think it might be best, to do one thing at a time."

"I'm sure you are right, Edward."

"I don't know how long the death certificate business will take, but I'm certain it won't be long before we meet again. Bye, Robert."

"Bye, Edward."

Edward arrived home about mid-day. Julian and Caroline met him in the lounge.

"How did you get on, Edward?" Julian asked.

"I gave Robert a list of changes that I feel should be made and included an account of why those changes should be made. However, as the original death certificate was obtained fraudulently, there is a possibility that it would be classed as illegal and invalid, which could mean complications, to say the least."

"What time scale are we talking about?" Caroline asked.

"Who knows, with all the unknowns, it could be a week or as long as several months. Meanwhile, Elizabeth, would you phone PC287 and arrange a meeting with him at the library with you and Jane. I shall then join you after he has entered the meeting."

Elizabeth went up to the study to phone PC287.

"Do you want us to attend that meeting with you Edward?" Julian asked. "Not at this point in time, I think it would be a good idea that PC287 is ignorant of your involvement in the wine-scam operation; he may have a suspicion that you're up to something, but if we have to, we can say you're looking into your father's death, which is the truth."

The meeting was arranged for the following Wednesday.

"Hallo, Peter, come through to the interview room," Jane invited.

After they entered the interview room and made themselves comfortable, Edward arrived and entered the room.

"What are you doing in here," demanded PC287.

"Trying to save you from a long prison sentence," Edward replied, bluntly. "We are going to ask you to help us, along with the help of my wife, Elizabeth, and her friend the chief librarian, Jane, to devise a plan as to how we can organise a raid on the building, to get it shut down permanently."

"Hopefully, we will also capture the operators; one of which is yourself, and I'm sure you will supply the names of the other two."

Chapter 27

"I think the best way to start," said Edward, "is for you, Peter, to give us the names and addresses of the two others, who we know are involved in this scam. Is that all right by you, Peter?"

"I'll take notes," suggested Jane.

"Right, the first one I think you know. Mr Hewson, who lives at the 'Bank House' in Church Lane. The second is a Monsieur Dupont, who, from his accent, is French and lives somewhere in Peterborough. Unfortunately, I don't know where. However, M. Dupoint is the wine expert and controls the taste of the wine."

"It's then loaded onto a barge and taken somewhere to be pack into cases; I don't know where that is though. A shipment is made about every six weeks. I'm just a dogs-body and do most of the humping about. Mr Hewson mixes the various cheap wines and chemicals together, according to M. Dupoint's recipe."

"Then, after M. Dupoint has approved the taste of the batch, Mr Hewson bottles it and sticks the appropriate labels on."

"When would all three of you be together?" Edward inquired.

"Usually, when we send a shipment out; at other times, we are normally by ourselves, although occasionally there could be two of us, depending on what needs doing, but that's not very often."

"Changing the subject for just a moment, there's a question I've been meaning to ask you, Peter," said Elizabeth. "When we first knew you, you were a bit of an arrogant, insolent bully, to say the least. However, now you are helpful, calm and dare I say it, nice! My question is: what happened to cause this dramatic change, for the better?"

"Well, I will try to explain it, but it may sound a bit farfetched. I don't know if you are aware that I used to be married and at that time I was quite placid. After a few years of marriage, my wife started to nag me to be more forceful."

"Over the following years I became, how did you put it— 'an arrogant, insolent bully'. Later on, she had an affair with Mr Hewson, but it only lasted for about a year and then he dumped her; consequently, I divorced her."

"Does she now run the post office?"

"Yes, after that, I couldn't see the point of changing. It wasn't until I made that clumsy attempt to pick you up, that I realised not every woman is like my ex-wife. From then on, I'm trying to revert to my old self."

"Thank you for telling me your story, and, Peter, you are succeeding very well."

"I appreciate your encouragement. Although, an opportunity to correct some of the wrongs Mr Hewson has done will provide me with some satisfaction. Although, I can't see how to undo the devastating effects he had on the Hewson family."

"What devastating effects were they, Peter?" Edward asked.

"Because I made Mr Hewett's death look like suicide, Mr Hewson was able to purchase 'Bank House' for virtually nothing and got Mr Hewett's family slung out onto the street. In addition, he got me in a position that would insure I had no option but support and protect his wine-scam from discovery."

"By helping get this wine-scam shutdown, you are on the way to help rectifying some of those effects."

"The only way I can think of bring the wine-scam to a permanent close, is by raiding the building during a shipment of wine, as it's the only time when we would all be there together; plus, you would be able to catch us with the goods, so to speak. Be warned though, Mr Hewson usually carries a gun during a shipment loading."

"That is a very useful observation, thank you. Can you suggest a way of notifying the raiding team when a shipment would be taking place. I think a minimum of twenty-four hours would be necessary for them to get prepared for the operation?"

"Judging from when we last made a shipment, the next one will be in about two to three weeks."

"I will need to speak with the chief constable to arrange how this is going happen. We'll call it a day for now and Elizabeth will arrange another get together, hopefully, in the not too distant future. Thanks for your input, Peter, and take care, because if the other two find out you have switched to the side of justice, they probably won't treat you with kindness."

"Thanks, Edward, Elizabeth and Jane, see you soon." With that, Peter left.

"I'm going back to the house," announced Edward. "Do you want to come with me?"

"I can't leave until about two o'clock," announced Jane.

"I'll go home with Edward, and you can come and join us when you have finished here."

"That sounds good to me. I'll let you both out the back door and join you at your house later."

"Welcome home, both of you, how did your meeting with PC287 go?" Julian asked.

"I'll be with you in just a moment," Edward said, as he went upstairs.

"I'm going to make Edward a coffee, do you two want one?"

"Yes, please," Julian and Caroline answered in unison.

"I'll let Edward tell you about the meeting," Elizabeth told them, as she brought the drinks in.

Edward joined them. "Now what would you like know," he said with a big smile.

"It must have been successful, judging from your big smile," Caroline commented.

"It certainly was. Peter told us the names of the other two involved; Mr Hewson, who we guessed was involved, and a Monsieur Dupont, who lives in Peterborough and is French, which you may have surmised from his name. Peter also suggested the best time to raid the building and catch them, was whilst they were making a shipment, which involves loading the wine bottles onto a barge."

"I have just made an appointment with the chief constable to organise a task force to raid the building with no windows and close the wine-scam down permanently."

"Do you think it will work?" Julian asked.

"The only way to find out is to attempt a raid. I'm going to see the chief constable tomorrow, in order to see how we can organise some of the details to make a raid."

It was quite late on Thursday evening when Edward returned from Grantham. Consequently, it wasn't until the Friday morning that he had a chance to explain the outcome of his meeting.

"Good morning, Edward," Julian said, as Edward came into the lounge. "We've had breakfast, but I'm sure Elizabeth will be able to satisfy your needs."

"I think she will," Edward replied, with a big grin.

"Here you are, dear, here's your breakfast," Elizabeth announced, handing Edward a tray.

"While you are all here, Robert has started putting together a raiding team which will include an armed response team. They will be on standby until we know the date of the wine shipment."

"What shall I tell Peter?"

"As soon as he knows the date of the shipment, he must let us know immediately. Inform him that he must take his usual part in the shipment and allow himself to be arrested. However, when they start to interrogate him, he must state that he wants a solicitor present; he's to give them my name and not to answer any questions until I'm with him at the police station."

"Edward, we need to go home to sort somethings out, I think now would be a good time. Then you could phone us

when your raid has been completed. What do you think?"
Julian inquired.

"That would be a good idea. It would avoid the chance of any embarrassing incidents."

Chapter 28

It was just over a fortnight later that Julian and Caroline received a phone call informing them that the raid had taken place and had been resounding success. And it was now safe for them to go back to Lower Darston.

In due course, they pulled in to the carpark of the Manor House, at about three o'clock on Saturday afternoon.

Elizabeth and Edward were standing on the doorstep before they had time to get out of the car. "Welcome back both of you, we have missed you. Come in, Edward will get your luggage. Go straight into the lounge and I'll make you some coffee."

"We can't wait to hear how your raid went," mooted Caroline.

"The raid started about eleven o'clock in the evening," Edward started the account, after sipping his coffee. "We watched from upstairs, so as to not get in the way, or even get shot."

"Don't be so dramatic," scalded Elizabeth.

"To continue, they were loading the bottles of wine onto the barge at the rate of about four bottles at a time. They had been at it for about ten minutes when the first police team arrived. Mr Hewson pulled a gun, but was immediately confronted by half-a-dozen armed police pointing their guns at him, and subsequently he surrendered and was led away."

"Peter allowed himself to be taken away. M. Dupoint tried to deny he was involved but he too was led away. A second police team boarded the barge and arrested the crew. Next morning, the barge was towed away and an investigative team started working on the contents of the building."

"What happened to Peter?" Caroline asked.

"Later that morning, I got a phone call from the local police station informing me that a Peter Robinson was being interrogated and had demanded I be present before he would answer any questions, so would I go and represent him at the police station, which is what I did."

"After they spent an hour or so interrogating him, eventually they were convinced he was with the police and had infiltrated the wine-scam gang. After Robert confirmed Peter was with the police, subsequently, they released him."

"I told him it might be advisable to disappear for a couple of weeks, which I assume he has done."

"It must have been an intense interrogation, as Edward didn't get back until late Thursday evening," added Elizabeth.

"I bet you were relieved the operation was completed satisfactory," commented Julian.

"We both were."

"I've invited Jane over for dinner, so I better get started on it," Elizabeth announced, as she disappeared into the kitchen.

"Another thing you should know is that Robert phoned me on Friday," continued Edward, "and told me something that will make you two very happy. He has just received a new death certificate for your father, indicating that he was killed by a person or persons' unknown."

"Hooray, at last we have started to make progress in finding out who killed Dad," Caroline whooped.

"Don't get too excited, we don't even know who killed him yet," warned Julian. "In fact, all we know is according to Aunt Lily, that he was taken ill during the evening before Dad died. We don't even know if he made it home that night."

At that point, the door-bell rang. "That will be Jane, I expect," said Edward, as he got up to answer the door.

"Hallo, Julian and Caroline," announced Jane, as she entered the room.

"How are you, Jane," replied Caroline. "It seems such a long time since we've seen you."

"I assume Edward and Caroline have told you about the excitement we've had while you were away," inquired Jane.

"Yes, he certainly has."

"Has Edward also told you his other news?" "No. Edward?"

"I have borrowed that legacy document from Jane and started work on getting your house back. Though I have yet to find a judge, who will be willing to take it on. But it's early days yet."

"Elizabeth, do you think we could arrange another meeting with Aunt Lily?" Julian asked.

"I'll try for next week. What do you want from her?"

"I want to know if she actually saw Dad go into his house."

Wednesday morning saw Elizabeth, Julian and Caroline on the door-step of number three Church Lane.

Elizabeth knocked on the door. the door was opened by Lily Jones. "Come in, Elizabeth," said Lily, "and of course you, Julian and Caroline. I still find it difficult think of you two as adults, and not small children. Go and sit in the parlour while I get some tea."

"Thank you, Lily."

A few moments later, the tea arrived. "Help yourselves," instructed Lily. "Thanks."

"What way can I help you?" Lily asked, with a disarming smile on her face. "Well, do you remember telling Elizabeth that you had seen Dad staggering home the evening before his death," asked Julian. "Yes, of course."

"Please could you cast your mind back and see, if you can remember seeing Dad actually getting inside 'Bank House'?"

"No, sorry, I can't. Because of the curve in the road, it's impossible to see 'Bank House' from the door or front room window of this house. Maybe you can from the other side of the road, I don't know."

"Is there anything you can remember from that evening?" Elizabeth inquired in a gentle voice.

"Let me think. Your dad staggered past here, I just happened to see him through the window. The curtains were open and the light shone on his face, which looked ghastly. I rushed to get the front door open, but by the time I got it open, it was locked with the security chain on, he had progressed to about number five or six, then I lost sight of him."

"Assuming he had made it home, I started closing the door. Hang on, I've just remembered. As I was closing the door a car came passed, as if it was going to the church. Although, I'm sure it was just a coincidence, and nothing to do with the death of your dad."

"About how long after Dad had passed, did the car come passed," asked Julian.

"One or two minutes at the most."

"Do you think the car would have caught up with Dad before he got home?"

"I haven't looked at it like that before, most certainly it could have, considering the speed the car was going. That means your dad could have been kidnapped before he got home."

"Exactly, although it's only supposition, it's a possibility we can bear in mind," Julian concluded.

"I'm sorry for not remembering before."

"Thank you for remembering it now. Anyway, we must thank you for the help and hospitality," concluded Elizabeth.

Chapter 29

"How did you get on?" Edward asked, when the three of them got back to the 'Manor House'.

"We discovered something new that Lily managed to recall, whilst we were chatting," replied Elizabeth.

"What was that?"

"After John Henry Hewett staggered passed Lily's house, literally within a second or two at the most, a car shot past it, as if going to the church, which raises the possibility that John could have been kidnapped before he had managed to reach his house."

"If we put all these coincidental happenings together, we have John Henry Hewett staggering home about eleven o'clock, sometime after being poisoned. However, somewhere between Aunt Lily's house and 'Bank House', he was hijacked by a car and taken to the church, probably using a copy of the church's key to open the door, where John's body was dumped in the Bell Ringing Chamber, which is where it was found the next morning," summed up Julian.

"That was well summed up, Julian," commended Edward. "All we have got to do now is discover: where and by whom John was poisoned."

"Well, as you are our wonder legal person, it should only take you a day or two to find that out," Caroline said facetiously, with a big smile on her face.

"Before this descends into violence, what do you want for lunch?" Elizabeth asked.

Thursday started pleasantly enough. Edward was up in his study, putting the legal documentation together for the reposition of 'Bank House'. The other three were finishing their late breakfast and putting the world to rights. Unexpectedly, the blissful atmosphere was shattered by the phone ringing.

"Who's that?" Elizabeth exclaimed, as she got up to answer the phone. "Hallo."

"O' it's you, Jane...no we not doing anything important, why?...Edward is busy, but we will be at the back-door in about fifteen minutes. Bye."

"Right on your feet, Jane wants us at the library to see something important."

"Did she say what it was?" Caroline asked.

"No, just that it's important."

Elizabeth went and told Edward where they were going and then the three of them set of for the library.

"Come in," said Jane, after she had opened the library back-door.

"What has made you so excited?" Julian asked.

"Come through to my office."

They followed her through to her office and sat round her desk. "Do you remember finding an invoice at the bank when you went through the archives stored in the bank?" Jane asked.

"Vaguely," replied Julian. "I thought it was interesting, rather than significant."

"That's what I thought at first. But when I found the invoice didn't say what it was invoicing for and that it was addressed for the attention of Mr Cole," continued Jane. "Consequently, I wrote to the company who sent the invoice, asking them to clarify what it was for. It took some time before they replied, which arrived in this morning's post."

"What did they say?" Julian asked.

"This is the reply," Jane said, pushing an A4 envelope towards them, take a look at the contents of this letter. "Unusually, I had to sign for it."

Julian took the contents from the envelop and scanned them. "Wow!" He exclaimed. Then he handed the contents to Elizabeth.

Caroline looked over Elizabeth's shoulder as she read through the documents.

Once Elizabeth had finished reading, she placed the documents back on Jane's desk.

"So what would a bank manager want with a hundred grams of Thallium Sulphate?" Jane asked.

"Or more interestingly, what would Jeremiah Cole want with a hundred grams of Thallium Sulphate?" Julian vehemently cried.

"Be careful, Julian," warned Caroline, "we only have circumstantial evidence linking Mr Cole to Dad's death. We need Edward to confirm that this evidence is strong enough to stand up in court."

"Let me copy this letter just in case the original goes missing, then you can take it to show Edward," Jane said, as she went across to the copier.

Jane then filed the copies in a filing cabinet, gave the originals to Julian and showed them out of the back-door.

"What was so important for Jane to call you over to the library?" Edward asked.

"Take a look at the contents of this letter," instructed Julian, handing Edward the A4 envelope.

A few minutes passed, as Edward examined the contents of the envelope.

"Well, well. That certainly is interesting," Edward finally commented. "But unfortunately it doesn't prove that Mr Cole actually killed your father."

"However, it certainly places him on the list of possible suspects. What we need is a motive. At the moment, we cannot find any reason for him to want your father dead; at least one that will stand up in court anyway."

"Does that mean we can't prosecute him for murder?" Caroline asked.

"If we did, there is, without a motive, a high possibility that he could be found not-guilty. However, with a motive, the jury would be difficult to persuade he didn't kill him."

"At this point, I cannot think of any plausible motive," responded Julian, with a disappointed note in his voice.

"Don't lose hope, Julian, although we know he is probably the killer, even we don't know one hundred percent. Consequently, we can look at what we know in a different light, maybe we have over looked something which would have lead us in some way to a motive we haven't thought of; or even to another possible killer."

"Like who?"

"That's what we have got to look into."

"I'll make some coffee," Elizabeth said as she went into the kitchen.

Coffee duly arrived, but everyone sat in silence as they drank their drinks.

"We have to go home to resolve some business situations that have arisen during last week; I think now would be a good time to do that, as it would help clear our minds. What do you think, Edward?" Julian asked.

"I actually think that is a very good idea actually," replied Edward. "It would give me a chance to finalise the reposition of 'Bank House'."

"Good, we'll leave first thing in the morning."

The afternoon of the next day saw them back in their own flats. Over the following week, the business issues were resolved satisfactory.

"Julian, are you in there?" Caroline called through the letter box in Julian's flat.

"Yes, come in, I'll make a drink."

"Sit down, I have something important to tell you."

"What's that?"

"I bumped in to Veronica, my genealogist friend, she said that George Hewett's daughter, Anne Lily Hewett, did marry."

"Who to?"

"Hold on to your hair—it was an Isaiah Cole. Not only that, they had a child who they named Jeremiah Cole. Veronica didn't think it was important, so didn't phone it through and just waited until we bumped into each other."

After a few seconds silence, Julian exclaimed, "That's the motive we've been looking for!"

"That's exactly what I thought."

"I'll phone Edward at once."

After phoning Edward, Julian announced, "We are leaving for the 'Manor House' in the morning. Is that alright by you?"

"Most certainly."

Chapter 30

Julian and Caroline were seating in the lounge at the 'Manor House'.

"Before moving onto your news, Elizabeth and I have something to tell you, which we hope you will be pleased with," announced Edward.

Edward went over and took an envelope from the small side table and handed it to Julian.

"Look at what's in there," Edward instructed Julian.

Opening the envelope, Julian found is contained a small bunch of keys, with a label tied on them.

Julian gasped and read the label out-loud. "These keys are for the 'Bank House' and belong to Julian and Caroline Hewett."

Julian and Caroline stared at Edward in disbelief.

"Yes, you now own the 'Bank House' and it's empty, waiting for you to move in."

"But it's in the name of Hewett."

"Yes, that is the name on the house's deeds, which I have upstairs in my office waiting for you to pick up. The legal team I set up said that Mr Hewson didn't object when they explained to him in his prison cell what would happen, he even arranged his family's removal."

"Mr Hewson was not told who the new owners would be, only that it had been discovered that Mr John Hewett was murdered and did not commit suicide. He immediately understood the implication of that discovery and didn't argue. But I don't know if he guessed that members of the Hewett family would be taking possession."

"I'm astonished how quickly the house business has been resolved," commented Caroline.

"To tell you the truth, so are we. I was expecting a drawn out legal battle. But because Mr Hewson didn't contest the finality of the legacy, it boiled down to a simple transference of the land registry details, which took about a week."

"Are you pleased with getting the house?" Elizabeth asked. "We wondered as you were so young when you lost the house and then left the village, if you would have emotional difficulties going back there."

"I don't know about Caroline, but for myself, I've not got any problems at the moment, but I'm not sure how I will feel when I go into the house itself and the distant memories come flooding back. What about you, Caroline?"

"I agree, but I think it will depend how much the inside has been changed. But I'm pleased that we have the opportunity to go and explore the reality of the dim memories I have got about the house. However, I have concerns about how the village is going to react, about having Hewett's back in the village."

"Well, I had similar thoughts," announced Elizabeth. "So I asked PC287 to discreetly inquire around the village how they would feel if a Hewett returned to live in 'Bank House. He found that the majority didn't have a view on the matter.

A small group said they wouldn't mind provided the Hewett's had nothing to do with the bank itself."

"So I think your concerns about the villager's attitude are unfounded. I think that going to view the house in the morning would be a good idea. What do you think."

"Yes, I think it's a good idea as well. What about you, Julian?"

"I'm fine with that. Now, would you like to hear our news now, Edward?" Julian asked.

"I most certainly would."

"Remember when we discussed the probability of Mr Cole being found guilty for dad's murder without him having a motive and there was some doubt as to whether or not Mr Cole would be found guilty."

"Yes, I remember."

"Well," said Caroline, "my friend, Veronica, the genealogist, she has been doing further research on George Hewett's family tree and found that his daughter, Ann Lily Hewett, married an Isaiah Cole, and in due course they had a baby son and named him Jeremiah Cole, the now bank manager, which makes Mr Cole the grandson of George Hewett; who was extremely upset that his father had cut him off without a penny."

"Now if George was continuingly ranting and raving about how aggrieved he was about not receiving any inheritance to his daughter and grandson, eventually, having to work with one of the Hewett's who had received benefit of the original inheritance, the desire to gain revenge for his grandfather has got to be overwhelming, which lead to the death of our father."

"That's wonderful!" Edward exclaimed. "I'll phone and make an appointment with Robert."

The next morning was full of excitement tinged with apprehension, as they climbed into Edward's car and drove the short distance to 'Bank House'. Having parked outside the front of the house, they sat looking at the outside for several moments, not knowing what to expect when they opened the front door.

"Come on, I've got the keys," said Julian, clambering out of the car. "I'm coming," called Caroline.

Elizabeth and Edward were close behind.

Julian stood outside the front door and inserted the appropriate key in the lock. "It's a bit on the stiff side," he said as he turned the key and pushed the door open.

They filed into the hallway.

"Have you missed us house? We have come to reclaim you after all these years," announced Caroline. "Julian, can you remember the layout of the house?"

"No, not really. We'll just have to go through one room at a time."

"Let's start by going through that door over there on the left," said Caroline, as she took the lead through the door and the others followed.

All four of them worked their way through the rooms on the ground floor and then returned to the hallway to go up the stairs to the upper floor, which they toured round. Having examined all the rooms in the house, they decided to return to the 'Manor House'.

"What did you think of the house?" Elizabeth asked, once they had settled in the lounge at the 'Manor House'.

"A new kitchen has been fitted and the upstairs and downstairs bathrooms have been refurbished. Apart from those, it seemed to be much as I remember," replied Caroline.

"It's decor is certainly satisfactory to live in," concurred Julian. "But as to if or when we would want take up residency, is another question we will need to resolve as soon as possible."

"That seems fair enough," Edward, agreed. "As for me, I'm going to Grantham in the morning to see Robert about the prospect of getting Mr Cole arrested, for the death of your father. You both are welcome to come with me."

Julian and Caroline looked at each other, and then Julian responded, "Thanks for the offer, Edward, but Caroline and I have a lot to discus and resolve, so I think we will be staying here."

"That's fine, Elizabeth will be here, so you will be able to come and go as you like."

After breakfast the next morning, Edward left for Grantham and Elizabeth shut herself upstairs, which left Julian and Caroline alone in the lounge.

"Have you got any thoughts on whether or not it would be a good idea to move here?" Julian asked Caroline.

"I think living in this village would be very nice. Although, moving away from where we were brought up could be a bit of a wrench. Do you think our business interests would transfer to this part of the country?"

"That's an interesting thought, I hadn't thought of that."

"Also, what's the internet speed like? I tend to use it mostly when I'm working."

"The mobile signal at 'Bank House' is quite strong, it was five bars on my phone when we were there, so communications shouldn't be a problem."

"We only need to sell one of the flats and keep the other one to use if we ever need to go visiting down south. Also, we would need to buy at least one car, as public transport is virtually non-existent in this area."

"Perhaps a more fundamental question is: can we live together in the same house, albeit a large house?"

"If we found we couldn't live together; we could always divide the house into two flats."

"I think that would be a shame, as it would spoil the symmetry of the building."

"Considering how many have helped us resolve our mystery, I think they would be little bit disappointed if we didn't move into the house. I know, let us go and talk to Jane, just to see what she feels."

"That sounds a good idea."

Julian phoned Jane to check she was available.

"She said she will unlock the backdoor in five minutes."

After letting Elizabeth know where they were going, they left for the library.

"Come in," Jane said, as she opened the library's backdoor for them. "Come through to my office. Now, what can I do for you?"

"I don't know if you are aware, but we now own 'Bank House', what we would like to know is what the villagers would think about having a Hewett living back in the house?"

"I have had quite a few come into the library and ask if it was true that the Hewett family were moving back into 'Bank House'. When I told them that the Hewett's now owned the

217

house, but didn't know if you were going to live there, ninety percent said it would be nice to have the old family back in residence."

"In fact, only one said it would be a bad thing and that was Mrs Robinson. To add my personal opinion, I will love you to move in. But it must be your personal decision."

"Thanks, Jane, for your help; we'll go back to the 'Manor House' now and try to make a decision about what we'll be happy doing."

"Come on, I'll let you out the backdoor."

"Thanks, see you later."

As they walked down the path towards the 'Manor House', Caroline said, "Hang on a moment. Everyone we've asked thinks us moving into 'Bank House' is a good idea. But what about us; what do we individually think? For example, what do you, Julian, personally think about moving into 'Bank House'?"

Julian stared her. "What do you mean, what do I think about moving into 'Bank House'?"

"Do you, Julian, want to live in 'Bank House'? Yes or no? It's not a difficult question."

"What do you want to do?"

"No, I want to hear what you want to do, without being influenced by someone else."

"I haven't really thought about it. I just assumed we were."

"That is exactly what I mean. We are not moving from this spot until you have thought about it and told me what you really want to do. For your information, I made my mind up whilst we were walking round the house earlier, and that is what I'm going to do, whatever you chose to do."

"So whatever I decide to do, whether I chose to live there or not; you will do what you've decided."

"Exactly!"

With that, Caroline sat on the grassy bank at the edge of the path. Julian stood looking at Caroline, trying to guess what she had decided.

The sun came out and Caroline dozed off. Time drifted by as Julian searched his conscience trying to decide what he really wanted to do. He hadn't realised how much his mind had been influenced by the expectations of others.

The sun started to wane. The cooling temperature caused Caroline to return to the land of the living. Julian was now sitting on the same grassy bank as Caroline. Julian became aware that Caroline was awake.

"Are you awake?" Julian asked.

"Yes. Have you made a decision?"

"Yes, but I'm not telling you, because it won't affect what you want to do."

"Touché, and I won't tell you what mine is. That way we won't be tempted to change our minds."

"Come on, it will dinner time shortly and we don't want to be late."

Chapter 31

The next morning at breakfast, Julian asked, "How did you get on at Grantham, Edward?"

"It was a bit involved, as we had to get in touch with the Crown Prosecution in order to establish if we had enough provable evidence to ensure we would in all probability get a conviction. Robert has put the case into the hands of a detective team to coordinate the evidence and arrange the arrest of Mr Cole. He will be in touch when he has a date for the court hearing."

Elizabeth suddenly asked, "What have you two decided in relation to 'Bank House'? You spent all of yesterday morning in consultation with Jane. She phoned to let me know when you left, but you didn't get back here until early evening; would you be upset if I ask were you were?"

"No, not at all, we were sitting on a grassy bank about halfway between the library and here and to make you even more curios, we sat in silence for most of that time," Julian answered.

"What decision did you arrive at?"

"One of the following four: Caroline stays and I go; I stay and Caroline goes; we both stay; we both go. We have each made our own choice, but we haven't told each other.

However, we have made a decision to hold a get together at the 'Bank House' this Saturday morning, which we would like you two to organise for us, under our guidance, where all will be revealed."

"What sort of get together had you in mind?" Edward asked.

"I think a buffet style would be suitable. You can get some caterers to sort the food and drink out. I think it should start at about ten o'clock."

"For how many people?" Elizabeth asked. "Here is a list:

You two.
Aunt Lily at number three Church Lane.
The family living at number one Church Lane.
Peter Robinson.
Jane Perry.
Robert.
Us two."

"And anyone you can think of who has helped to resolve our quest."

"I make that ten persons, which doesn't seem very many," commented Edward.

"As I just said," said Julian, "if there is anyone else you can think of, who has helped us in some way with our quest, please invite them."

"Well, both Edward and I are intrigued by what will be revealed on Saturday."

Both Julian and Caroline smiled mischievously at them, and Julian asked, "Is it alright if we continue to stay here?"

"Of course it is," answered Elizabeth.

Over the few days before Saturday, the four of them were busy booking the caterers and decided what drinks were required and appropriate food. They then organised the chairs in a layout so their occupants would be easily able to see Julian and Caroline when they were speaking.

By now, it was fairly late on Friday night. Julian and Caroline were at the top of the stairs, on their way to bed, when they heard Edward's phone rang. "Hallo…yes, Robert, it is Edward…really, and what did he have to say for himself…O' that is good news. Thank you, Robert."

Saturday morning saw them all getting ready. They had decided to leave at nine fifteen.

A few moments later, they arrived at the 'Bank House'. Opened the front doors and let the caterer's in, Julian and Caroline went upstairs to get ready. At about five to ten, the first guests started to arrive and Edward and Elizabeth welcomed them and showed them where they should be seated.

Eventually, all the expected guests were seated. Elizabeth went upstairs to tell Julian and Caroline all was ready and went back down stairs and took her seat.

A few moments later, Julian and Caroline came down the stairs and stood in front of the gathered audience.

"Thank you all for coming this morning. In one way or another, you have all helped Caroline and myself to resolve a mystery that began some twenty plus years ago, with the death of our father," began Julian.

"Along the way, we helped the police break up a major wine scam gang, which lead to this house being returned to its legal owners; us. Now I'm sure you are all dying to know who is going to live here. We have two envelopes here, one from

Caroline and one from me, which I am going to ask Edward Blackmore to open."

Edward stood up and walked over and took the envelopes from Julian. "This envelope is Julian's, which reads: 'Over the time we have been staying in this village, I have fallen in love with it'. Consequently, I'm going to live in 'Bank House' for the foreseeable future."

"The second envelope is Caroline's, which reads: 'I have enjoyed staying in Darston, thus I'm going to live here in 'Bank House'."

The audience burst into spontaneous applause.

"That's not all," Edward continued. "Late last night I received a phone call from the chief constable in Grantham, who told me that they had arrested Jeremiah Cole on suspicion of murdering John Henry Hewett. However, when they started questioning him and presented him with the evidence, he confessed."

"So as Julian said earlier, about you all helping in one way or another, we all have solved the mystery of the 'Hanging Banker'. I'm now going to hand back to Julian."

"As you may or may not know, is that Caroline and my name is Hewett. This will come as a shock to some in the village. We hope that we can reassure those who are worried about it, and that all the upsets from the past will remain in the past. Also be assured, that any connections that were with the bank have now been severed."

"There is food and drinks in the other room, so please go and enjoy yourselves."